Fleabiscuit Sings!

Fleabiscuit Sings!

Marlene Fanta Shyer

Marshall Cavendish

New York · London · Singapore

Text copyright © 2005 by Marlene Fanta Shyer
All rights reserved
Marshall Cavendish, 99 White Plains Road, Tarrytown, NY 10591
www.marshallcavendish.us
Library of Congress Cataloging-in-Publication Data
Shyer, Marlene Fanta.
Fleabiscuit sings! / by Marlene Fanta Shyer.
p. cm.
Summary: A down-on-their-luck New York City family thinks they can make some money
when they discover that their neighbor's dog can sing harmony in the family's subway singing
act.
ISBN 0-7614-5213-3
[1. Dogs—Fiction. 2. City and town life—New York (State)—New York—Fiction. 3. Family
life—New York (State)—NewYork—Fiction. 4. New York (N.Y.)—Fiction.] I. Title.
PZ7.S562F1 2005
[Fic]—dc21
2004019454

This book is set in Stempel Garamond.
Book design by Anahid Hamparian
Printed in The United states of America
First edition
6 4 2 1 3 5 7

To Alice Ridley, who should be singing on
Broadway instead of under it,
also, to A.J., who would much rather carry a bone
than a tune

one

It all began the summer my best friend,
Ziggy, moved away. The day was so hot there was a
cat running through the open hydrant down at the
end of the block. It was too steamy to shoot baskets
or practice my xylophone, and ever since our computer had a meltdown, it was good-bye to my PC
games. So there I was, sitting on my stoop getting a
pebble out of my shoe and trying to figure out what
to do next when someone called out to me.

"Hey, fella!" It was Mr. Moffat, who lives on
the fifth floor of building number 214, which is next
door to 216, where I live. All the kids call him Mr.
Muffin, not because he's short and shaped like one,
which he sort of is, but because he used to own a
bakery downtown. He is always baking something
or other that makes the whole block smell like
dessert. His face was poking out between two plants

in an open window. "Hey, fella!" he called again, and he waved at me to come up, which, of course, I didn't want to do. Five flights is seventy steps (I live on the fourth floor, fifty-six steps), but he kept waving at me like it was a matter of great importance. "Come up here a minute, willya?"

Step by hot step I climbed to where he was waiting for me at his apartment door. In one hand, he was holding a cookie in the shape of a hockey puck that glowed white as snow from the sugar he had rolled it around in. He was holding it between two fingers like it was made of gold. What got my attention, though, was the puppy that was squeezed under his other arm.

"This is Fleabiscuit," he said. The puppy had a fuzzy face, short legs, wet brown eyes, and two ears that folded over like the backs of envelopes. "I just now got him," Mr. Muffin explained, "because my granddaughter said she didn't want me living up here alone. Of course, she took him to the vet, got rid of the fleas first. Ever since I got my pacemaker, I'm supposed to exercise, not scratch! She thinks I'm gonna need company, but the joke's on her. I'll go out as soon as the weather cools off, but for now, it's too hot for me to walk this little guy." He pointed to his chest. "This here pacemaker has my heart keeping a sorta beat. Like not losing

2

rhythm. And you know all about that, right?"

He meant I should know about rhythm because my mother has the most beautiful singing voice in New York City and my father used to play the guitar before his accident. Also, my little sister, Maria Elena, is taking up the flute. We call her M.E. for short, which sounds like Emmie, which, I told Mama, is what should have been her name in the first place. Emmie thinks she's good at the flute, but I'm here to tell you she's really not. She can dance okay, though, and whenever Mama lets Emmie come with us to do our act, Emmie starts tapping her feet like they're on batteries and waving her arms like they're windmills, and people do clap.

All of us play for Music Under New York. We perform on the platforms in the subway, and people who are waiting for trains put money in a big basket my dad bought just for that purpose. I sometimes walk around trying to sell the tapes we've made, but I've never sold more than four or five in one day. I want to double that number to 9, my lucky number. If I ever sell that many in one afternoon I think I'll get my voice back. It's been creaking like a door in a haunted house since I turned twelve, and that was months ago.

During the summer, when it's too hot to be underground where there are no cool breezes,

Mama sells Italian ices on upper Broadway. She says she has no talent for it. It used to be Daddy's summer job before he died. What happened was that one day he went down to the basement in our old apartment to put in an amp fuse. He wanted to be able to play his electric guitar at the same time Mama was ironing clothes without the fuses blowing. They called it a short, but there should be a better name for it: He stepped in a little bit of water that had leaked from a pipe, there was a loud crack that we heard all the way upstairs, and he was electrocuted. We got stacks of letters and get-well cards from his students at Arthur Miller Junior High School, but he never did come back from the hospital. For a long time after he died, I dreamed about him being alive, then woke up mornings crying because he wasn't.

After Daddy's accident and after the money the lawyer got us was used up, we had to move in with Grandma. Uncle Travis lives with us, too. The week after Daddy died, my uncle lost control of the bus he was driving and hit the back of a police car. Although nobody on the bus was hurt, Uncle Travis lost his job. He said he crashed because he heard that big, loud firecracker noise in his head that reminded him of Daddy's death. Now he sits at the window, looking up at the stars at night and down at the street during the daytime. Sometimes he smokes, and once he found the watch Daddy bought for my birthday. He sold it to buy a carton of cigarettes, which made Mama almost as mad as it made me. Mama says I'll love him more when we get our own place. "A hedge between keeps friendships green," she says, but I'm not convinced. I also wish he wouldn't wear Dad's Road Runners cap with the little flying horse on the back. Even if Dad and Uncle Travis were brothers, the hat doesn't belong to my uncle. After sharing a room with him for as long as I have, I'm not sure he deserves to wear it at all.

two

Mr. Muffin handed me Fleabiscuit. "Just walk him up and down the street for a while, will ya, fella? When you bring him back, I'll give you one of these." He waved the cookie in the air like he was the Statue of Liberty waving her torch. "What's baked into it is a secret between me and the Man in the Moon. I've locked the recipe in a safe in the Chase Manhattan Bank on West Fourteenth Street. You've never in your life tasted anything like it. It's a Hope cookie."

"A *Hope* cookie?"

Mr. Muffin's laugh was like an echo of a laugh. "Yeah. If you eat one, you'll hope to eat another one!"

I carried Fleabiscuit down every step because his legs were still so short. The minute I got onto the street, Uncle Travis was at the window yelling down at me, "What's that you got, Nicky?" He watched as

I put on Fleabiscuit's leash. "Where'd you get that dog? Whose dog is that? What're you doing with him?" My sister joined him at the window in a flash, and before I even got to the corner, Emmie was right alongside me.

"Let me walk him!" she said all excited, like she'd never seen a dog in her whole life before. "He's so cute, so sweet, so *droll*!" *Droll* was her latest word, probably found on some sixth-grade spelling list on a school computer. Even though she is only seven, she is an excellent speller. She kept on ragging me, as if someone had turned a windup key in her back.

I told her to bug off, she was too young to help, which got her looking like she would fold right up and crumple to the sidewalk. So when Fleabiscuit stopped to examine the bottom of a United States post office mailbox, I let her hold the leash for a minute. She lit up right away. "Is-it-a-girl-is-it-a-boy-What's-his-name-Where'd-he-come-from?" and a whole string of other questions came pouring out of her.

Then, she was like Velcro, stuck to me every minute, and she begged me to walk Fleabiscuit to Broadway, where Mama was stationed with her ices.

We walked very slowly, since Fleabiscuit paused at every telephone pole and hydrant, and also because people kept stopping to admire him. He had a sort of *something* that made people want to bend down and take a closer look or pat his head. He was the color of a paper bag in some spots and white in others, and he had one little dot of black between his eyes, like a bull's-eye beauty mark. People would go *Oooh* and *Ohhh* and *What's his name?* every couple of feet.

Emmie and I walked and walked, trying to stay in the shade so Fleabiscuit's paws wouldn't get too hot from the pavement. Finally we spotted Mama up ahead.

As we got closer I could see she was really annoyed about something. She pointed to a long, shiny silver car by the curb. "Every day!" she said, putting her hands on her hips. "Every day, this man parks his car right in front of my cart!"

Mama has a license from the city to stand at a certain place at the corner and sell Italian ices. Cars have to stop there at the traffic light. Many of the drivers buy an Italian ice while they're waiting for the light to change. But when someone parks at the curb, the car hides the cart and Mama loses business.

"I told him yesterday! I told him the day before! I said, 'Move your car back a couple of feet,' but no! There it is again, cutting into my sales!"

Just then, the owner of the car appeared. He

was wearing a straw hat and a shirt that looked like birthday gift-wrapping paper. His eyes were the same color as Fleabiscuit's, but you had to really search for them under his dark eyebrows. Mama stepped right over to the car as he was getting in and tapped on the passenger-side window. He completely ignored her, started up the engine, and took off.

"Did you see that? He comes into Rick's Café every day for lunch and leaves his car sitting here for an hour. An *hour!*" Her face had turned pink in some spots and white in others. She was so distracted that it took her a while to notice Fleabiscuit. Emmie had picked him up, and he was play-biting her thumb. "He's Mr. Muffin's," she told Mama.

"Mr. Moffat's dog? Poor man. I hope he feels better soon. He's been really sick. He was in the hospital practically the whole month of June!"

"He's much better now." I told her about the pacemaker and explained he'd be giving me a Hope cookie for walking Fleabiscuit.

"A *what* cookie?" She was busy scooping out a lemon ice for me and a raspberry one for Emmie. Mama never forgets our favorite flavors.

"A Hope cookie," Emmie said. She'd gotten

that information out of me earlier. "Mr. Muffin's secret recipe."

"Save it for after dinner," Mama said. "We're having ravioli, and you can eat it for dessert."

three

I returned Fleabiscuit to Mr. Muffin, and he gave me the cookie. As soon as I got home, I put it on a green plate next to the toaster in the kitchen. But, when I went to get it, the plate was in the sink and the cookie was gone.

"Who ate it?" I demanded, walking into the living room, my voice climbing up and down and up again. As usual, no one heard me. That's one problem with living with Grandma, aside from my having to share a room with Uncle Travis, who snores, wears Dad's hat to bed, and sometimes yells out in his sleep. The TV has to be on full blast because although Grandma's ears look all right from the outside, they don't work so well on the inside.

"Who ate my *cookie*!" I repeated, in a very, very loud voice.

"Was that yours, Nicky?" Uncle Travis asked,

trying to look innocent. "I saw it lying there and I got carried away. I thought I'd just take one little bite—but boy, that was some cookie! I couldn't stop eating it!"

"You just went ahead and *ate* my cookie without even asking?" I was about to boil over when Uncle Travis let out a big ha ha and said he was kidding. He explained he only wanted to see my face turn colors and would he ever really do something like that to his favorite nephew? He'd obviously forgotten about my watch, but I hadn't. And if I was his favorite nephew, it's because I was his *only* one.

It took me a minute to calm down and when I did, he showed me where he'd hidden it. It was in a soup bowl on the top shelf of the cupboard near the sink. Then he asked me what the big deal was about one darn cookie, anyway?

So, with Uncle Travis all eyes, I took my first bite. Mr. Muffin's cookie did taste different, although there was nothing extraterrestrial about it. It was made of two sugary, buttery cookies stuck together with something chewy—something sort of like butterscotch and vanilla mystery cream in the middle. It was pretty good all right. I finished every bite and said, "Mmmm," and even licked my fingers.

I was still mad at Uncle Travis, so it felt good

to see his mouth water since he thought he'd missed the treat of a lifetime. "How was it?" he wanted to know.

"Awesome," I said, but a minute later, I felt a little guilty. "I'll try to get one for you tomorrow," I promised. Uncle Travis went back to the window to look up at the stars, but it was a cloudy night and there were very few. "I can't even see the Eagle Nebula," he complained.

"What's that?" Emmie wanted to know.

"It's a bunch of stars shaped sort of like an eagle, and at the tips of the wings you can see new stars. I'm looking for a special new celestial body," Uncle Travis told her.

I had heard this before, but maybe Emmie hadn't. I had heard about Eta Carinae, the galaxy Centaurus A, and the Crab Nebula. I'd also listened to him go on about Sirius, Vega, Canis Major and Minor. Uncle Travis thought a new star meant that Daddy had landed up in heaven and was looking down at us. It had been three years since he died, and my uncle imagined it took that long to get a soul up there, traveling at full speed.

"Does everyone who dies get a star?" Emmie wanted to know.

"Only the really sterling people," Uncle Travis said. Then he went on about how he wished he had a high-powered telescope. With a better view of the universe, he imagined he could find everyone's soul in the heavens, including Grandpa's and even George Washington's.

Of course, Emmie came up with her usual bunch of questions: Did souls get to watch DVDs and own PlayStations, and were they allowed to eat the breakfast cereals of their choice? Could they go on singing or playing the guitar?

Uncle Travis shrugged and said there were some questions to which he didn't have answers. Maybe if he got his hands on a good enough telescope, he could do better research.

Emmie never gives up. "What about dogs and cats? Do they get their own stars?" she wanted to know. "And how do you spell *sterling*?"

"I think I hear Grandma calling you," Uncle Travis said, squinting up at heaven. It was his way of getting rid of her.

Of course, Grandma was not calling Emmie. She was watching a TV show about alligators in Florida and embroidering initials on shirt cuffs. She does that better than anybody. She puts monograms wherever anyone wants them: on pockets or linen napkins or handkerchiefs. She can do big letters or small ones, plain or with curlicues, in any color of the rainbow. The department store people send her boxes of blouses and shirts and towels, sometimes even nightgowns and underwear. She puts on her glasses and goes to work with a thimble on her middle finger and a tape measure around her neck. She sewed my initials on my knapsack and Emmie's whole name on her backpack. When Ziggy moved to Florida, he gave him an initialed T-shirt as a good-bye present. Mama says it's a talent she was born with and it makes up for the fact that she can't hear well enough. *Maybe I could get her to put a monogram on Fleabiscuit's collar,* I thought. I'd promised to walk him again tomorrow afternoon, and as soon as Emmie heard that, she began begging for her own dog. That is what she's really good at: begging. Just a few weeks ago, she'd seen a pair of sneakers with little blinking red lights in the soles. She begged for them until Mama gave in and bought them for her. Now I was sure she'd never let up about getting a puppy. "Maybe when we get our own apartment," Mama told her with a sigh.

At night, as soon as Grandma goes to sleep, Mama sits in the living room and practices new songs. I hum along in my head but keep my mouth shut because when I try to join in, only squeaks come out. I like to lie awake and listen to her tapes of folk songs, gospel music, country songs, and even her favorites, the oldies, the ones that usually put me to sleep. Grandma says Mama's voice is like a ribbon of silver going through the air, and that's just about right. When I close my eyes and listen, I can practically see it, a shiny flutter, spinning like a pinwheel or floating slowly, above or below me, just out of reach.

That night, the night I ate the Hope cookie, I had another dream about Daddy that was very real. He was sitting on the stoop outside, playing his guitar and singing "Santa Lucia." Mama was up in the window, smiling. She actually has a tape Daddy made, but never plays it. "It's tears music," she says, but in my dream, I was sitting next to him and listening to all those Italian words I didn't understand and probably couldn't learn if I wanted to. I wasn't a bit sad; I was so happy to have him back and sitting next to me. And when the music ended, he put his arm around my shoulder and said there was something he had to tell me. The dream faded before he could, so I never did find out what it was.

The next morning, after Mama left, I practiced "Santa Lucia" on my xylophone again and again until I had it down pat. Well, almost.

four

I walked Fleabiscuit the following day and the day after that. Each time, Mr. Muffin gave me a Hope cookie. Uncle Travis said we should try to get the recipe either out of the Chase Manhattan Bank or from the Man in the Moon, ha ha. When I gave a cookie to Mama, she said Mr. Muffin certainly knew his business. She gave Emmie half, and my sister said she'd never eat a chocolate chip cookie again; these were much better. But when Grandma took a bite, she said she didn't know what all the fuss was about. She didn't think they were as good as the ones she used to bake before she began monogramming. Mama winked at me and whispered that Grandma's taste buds weren't what they used to be. Besides, Grandma was in one of her moods.

We call them Grandma's "black-thread days," when she clicks the remote control a mile a minute because she can't find anything she likes on TV. During those times, she doesn't like much that's not on TV either, including any of us. Grandma blames rainy days, when her "knees and everything above and below them hurt." Mama says that's not it. "She needs her space, and we're too much in it."

One day when Grandma was letting me have it for leaving wet towels on the floor, Emmie came up with an idea. "Let's bring Fleabiscuit over here to cheer her up," she said. Grandma had just yelled at Uncle Travis for letting out a loud one after eating a green apple. So he said, "If it takes a dog to cheer her up, I'm all for it."

By now Fleabiscuit and I had really clicked. I mean, as soon as I would arrive at Mr. Muffin's door, he'd be wagging not only his tail but his whole body. Then he'd jump and bounce around like a Super Ball, running circles around my ankles. He wouldn't let me put on his leash; he was too busy licking my hand. "Puppy kisses," Mr. Muffin said. "He's gone bananas over you." Very often Mr. Muffin would slip baking ingredients into his conversation.

So, on this rainy day, when Emmie suggested I introduce Fleabiscuit to Grandma, I carried him up to our apartment after walking him. Right away I put him in Grandma's lap. At first, it worked like a charm. Grandma's whole face picked itself up and it was like the sun had just rolled into the living room. Grandma scratched the top of Fleabiscuit's head and told him he reminded her of a dog she'd seen on a TV talk show.

But then she sneezed, and that made Fleabiscuit nervous. He started to shake, and his tail stopped wagging. Her sneeze was followed by another sneeze, and then another.

"Fleabiscuit's edgy," Uncle Travis said. Mama could see it right away, too. "I know just what will calm him down," she said, snapping her fingers in the air. "Music!"

Mama stood right in front of Fleabiscuit and started singing "Blue Skies." She sang softly at first, then worked up to her full-bodied, silver-ribbon sound.

Suddenly Fleabiscuit stopped shaking. He turned his head a bit to the side to listen, like he was hearing not just with his ears, but with his whole little self. Then, one of his envelope-flap ears, the left one to be exact, stood straight up in the air, pointing at the ceiling, at full attention.

"Did you see that?" Emmie's eyes were wide.

"I did. I surely did!" Grandma had covered her mouth with a monogrammed handkerchief to stop sneezing. "What we have here is a puppy music lover!"

But it turned out she didn't know the half of it, and of course, neither did we.

five

The very next day Mr. Muffin said that the sidewalks were hotter than cookie sheets that had just come out of the oven. He'd barely managed his early morning stroll to the corner. He suggested I walk Fleabiscuit only a short way. Then he asked me if I'd noticed a change. Had I seen that one of his ears was sticking straight up? "Straighter than a candle in a cake?"

"It was the music," I told him, and then explained about Mama's voice and its amazing magic.

"When bread rises in an oven, it's not because of music. It's not magic, either. It's *destiny*," Mr. Muffin said. "Same with Fleabiscuit. His ear was meant to rise, sooner or later."

I didn't want to argue with Mr. Muffin. I decided instead to take Fleabiscuit to Broadway and have Mama sing "Blue Skies" again. Maybe she could get the other ear to go up.

Emmie wasn't with me that day because a neighbor had invited her to the beach. And since she wasn't fighting with me for the leash, Fleabiscuit and I could walk a little bit faster. We got to Broadway in no time flat.

Mama was standing under the striped umbrella of her cart, scooping out balls of orange, lemon, cherry, and grape ice for a couple of kids from the neighborhood. Of course, they asked what kind of dog Fleabiscuit was and how come he had one ear up and one ear down and could he do tricks. I knew Fleabiscuit was one-of-a-kind. Everyone knows that if you check out a snowflake under a microscope, you'll see it's different from every other snowflake. I thought Fleabiscuit was like that: Other dogs might look like him, but none was an exact duplicate.

"He's a mutt, I bet," one kid said.

"Oh, no!" I answered right away. Although there is nothing wrong with being a mix of breeds, I didn't like the sound of the way the kid said "mutt." "He's a purebred Woodlawn Mountain Riff." It just popped out of me. Sometimes, when I make things up, I surprise myself. A *riff* is something Mama sings when she's improvising. *Woodlawn* is the name of the cemetery where Dad is buried. And since Fleabiscuit had started going up and down stairs, every step was still like climbing a mountain of butter. *Mountain* stuck in my head, which is why I'd said Woodlawn *Mountain* Riff.

The kids were impressed. "'Woodlawn Mountain Riff'?" they repeated. I hoped they wouldn't go home and check it out on the Web.

Just as Mama was scooping out some lemon ice to give to me, the same long, silver car that always blocked the corner pulled up at the curb.

Mama's face geared up. She plunked the scoop of lemon ice into a cup and handed it to me, all the while keeping an eye on the man who was climbing out of the driver's side. He was not wearing his straw hat today. He was dressed in a dark suit and black tie. She raised her scoop high, as if it were a flag she was about to wave, signaling troops to battle. "Excuse me, sir!" she said.

The man gave her a sort of a salute and waved a hand in the air. I thought it meant, "I don't want any Italian ice right now." He kept right on going.

"Excuse me, sir!" Mama called again, volume turned up, but the man swooshed by and into Rick's Café.

"Did you see that?" Mama's face was red, and it had nothing to do with the heat. "Did you *see* that?" she repeated. "He pays no attention to me whatsoever! It's like I don't exist! And look! Look where he parked his car. *Again!*"

She started biting her lip, which she does when she's thinking. Suddenly, she did the most un-Mama-like thing. It practically froze me to the sidewalk with surprise. She swung the ice scoop like she was about to swat a fly, then swooped it through the air and down into the raspberry ice. She dug out a huge blob of dark red ice and flipped it onto a napkin sitting on top of her cart.

Next thing, she picked up the napkin full of raspberry ice, walked over to the man's car, and smeared it across the windshield like it was something she did every day. She made big arcs on the glass, like my teacher cleaning chalk off the blackboard, back and forth, back and forth, until the entire windshield was covered with red ice. I think my mouth sort of hung open. Was this really happening or was I seeing things like those desert mirages? But the kids saw it too and were letting out loud cheers. "Go, Mrs. Valentin! Go! *Go!*" they yelled, whistling, applauding, stamping their feet, and jumping up and down like cheerleaders. "Right on! Yo! Get him! GO!"

I was too shocked to join in, but I was

absolutely thrilled . . . until I saw the owner of the car come out of the café. His face turned practically the color of the raspberry ice on his windshield. He headed right for Mama, at full speed.

six

I'd been holding Fleabiscuit under my right arm to give his paws a rest from the hot sidewalk. When the driver of the car started walking toward Mama, I put Fleabiscuit right down. In the dark suit and tie and without the straw hat, the man looked much bigger and scarier, sort of like the superintendent of the whole school system. I began to worry he might get rough with my mother. It sure looked that way. He was taking long steps, his hands rolled into fists, and there was fire in his eyes. The kids who'd gathered to eat Italian ice backed off and got quiet, waiting for whatever was going to happen, to happen.

"What the *badword* do you think you're doing!" was the first thing he said. His voice was so loud, even Grandma could have heard it at our apartment three blocks away. The man was practically nose-to-nose with Mama. "What the *badword*

did you do to my *car*?" His voice, which I didn't
think could get louder, came booming out of his
mouth. The door to the café opened, and two or
three people stepped out. I looked up and down the
street for a policeman, but no luck, none in sight.

"What right do you have, lady, to *badword* my
badword windshield? What the *badword* is wrong
with you?"

My mother put one hand on her hip. She
pointed the ice scoop at him with the other, and
then, she let the man have it. She told him he was
inconsiderate, thoughtless, mean, and disrespect-
ful. She told him that she was trying to make a living, and he was cutting into her business. She said
he was an insensitive so-and-so to park his car
just where it would block her automobile-passen-
ger sales. And she told him to watch his mouth;
didn't he see there were children here and that
they should not be exposed to this kind of language?

It seemed as if she'd calmed him down, but
then he started up again. He pointed his finger at
her and at the car and at the sky. He shouted that
he had to pick up a client at the airport and how
could he see to drive? How could he clean up this
mess? He waved his arms and stamped his feet.
He glared at Mama and Mama glared back. "Take

it easy, Roe," somebody from the café said. "You' gonna have a heart attack!"

Mama just stood there without moving until the man took out a big white handkerchief and wiped his forehead. He took a few steps back, and I could see he was trying to calm down. I guess Mama could see that, too, because all of a sudden she took her hand off her hip and bit her lip. Then, she opened the refrigerator door on top of her cart, pushed in the scoop, and pulled out a ball of orange ice. She stuck it into a cup and held it out to the man.

"Free of charge," she said.

He was speechless for a second. I could see he didn't know if he should accept it or not. Did he think Mama was trying to poison him? Finally, he reached out and took the cup. "Much obliged," he said. He stuck out his tongue to take a taste. "Not bad," he said. After a few more licks, he apologized for parking on Mama's corner. I love Mama's smile—it's practically melodious—and here it came. Next thing I knew, she and the man were shaking hands and Mama was apologizing for messing up his car.

It's hard to believe, but he and my mother struck up a conversation that was so friendly, you would have thought they'd been pals all their lives.

The kids standing around lost interest and moved off. Someone from the café brought out a bunch of wet paper towels, and the man parked his handkerchief—who would believe it?—on Mama's cart while he—and Mama!—cleaned his windshield together.

Next thing I knew, Mama was introducing me. The man's name was Roebuck, and he right away told me I had a mother who was "a doozy, but in the best sense." He hoped I was proud of her. He said she reminded him of his own mother, who could stand up to anybody and often did.

And then he noticed Fleabiscuit. I'd picked him up again and he was licking my face with puppy kisses. Roebuck patted his head and then Fleabiscuit began licking his fingers. "Nice pooch," he said. "It's funny how one ear is up and one's down, isn't it?"

Then I remembered why I'd come here in the first place, and I told him my mother could make his other ear stand up just by singing. Or at least, that was what had happened last time. Of course, Roebuck looked like he didn't believe a word of it, so I asked Mama to sing just a little bit of "Blue Skies."

But just then, two more customers arrived, and my mother got busy scooping out more Italian ices. Roebuck apologized for his bad language two or three times. Then he explained that he had to run out to the airport and he'd probably be back tomorrow. He promised, crossed his heart right over his dark suit jacket, that he'd never park on Mama's corner again.

And sure enough, he never did.

seven

The next day, Emmie and I decided to walk
Fleabiscuit back to Broadway. We wanted to try
again to get Mama to sing. On the way, Emmie
stopped dead in her tracks in the middle of the
street and said her head hurt. She wanted to turn
around and go right home. I'm not allowed to let
her go anywhere alone, so I had to turn around and
walk her back, listening to her complain every
minute of the way. She said she'd gotten too much
of something at the beach the day before, but she
wasn't sure what it was. Maybe it was the seaweed
in the water, the sun in the sky, or the oyster shell
she'd stepped on. When some people get sick, they
clam up; not my sister.

I told her loud and clear to be quiet for a
minute and look at Fleabiscuit. He'd grown bigger,
hadn't he? It suddenly looked as if his collar was

getting too tight. I kneeled down, checked it out, and decided to loosen it a notch. That was a mistake. In order to loosen it, I had to unfasten the thingy that latched the collar closed. The minute I did, disaster! Fleabiscuit wriggled out, dashed between my legs, and took off like I'd fired a starting gun. Emmie let out a yell that sounded like the world had come to an end. Someone shouted "HEY!", probably thinking Emmie was being kidnapped, but I had no time to explain. I took off after Fleabiscuit, and in more than twelve years of life, I've never run so fast. Fleabiscuit was a streak of lightning. He was the length of three big dogs ahead of me, and my heart was going like bongos. I was scared spitless he'd run out into the street and get run over.

Emmie, who'd forgotten her hurting head, shoulders, neck, and whatever else she'd been complaining about, came running after me, yelling, "Catch him, Nicky! Catch him!" What did she think I was doing—chasing butterflies? I nearly knocked over a lady walking with a cane. I almost ran into a kid delivering a bouquet of flowers big as an open parachute. Fleabiscuit was like an arrow, flying between people's legs, around a pushcart of ladies' pocketbooks, and right under a row of U.S. mailboxes. When he got to the corner, his dog guardian angel must have been watching over him, because just as he began to dash across the street, the light turned green and the *walk* sign flashed on. Fleabiscuit zipped over both curbs without being hit by a car, thank God. Then, suddenly, I lost sight of him.

"Where is he? Where is he?" It turns out Emmie runs better when she's sick than when she's not. She wasn't that far behind me. "He's gone!" she wailed, while I tried to catch my breath. "He's disappeared!"

As I said, my lucky number is 9, and what do you know? Fleabiscuit had braked to a stop smack behind a bunch of cartons being delivered to the 99-cent store. I crossed the street, and Emmie caught up to me. She said she now had a headache in her stomach, too. Meanwhile, Fleabiscuit looked as fresh and perky as ever, like he'd just come back from a vacation of air-conditioned naps.

A guy on a big motor bike was parked in front of the store, eating pizza. At first I figured Fleabiscuit had stopped to sniff the slice. That's what the man on the motor bike thought, too, because as soon as he spotted Fleabiscuit, he said, "Hey, pooch, you could smell the pie, huh?" But then I realized that that wasn't it. A portable radio was hanging off one handlebar. It was blasting out a song about a man on a highway heading nowhere.

The radio was practically bouncing with the sound, and it wasn't my imagination: The music coming out of that little yellow portable had attracted Fleabiscuit. Even when the man on the motor bike threw him a little piece of pizza crust, Fleabiscuit showed no interest. Instead, he got as close as he could to the little radio. Then he tilted his head to the side and began wagging his tail like it was electric.

Luckily, I managed to snatch him and get his collar back around his neck. I held the leash as tight as I could, breathing normal breaths again. Emmie grabbed my arm. "Look at his tail. Look at his face! He likes music!" Even she couldn't miss it.

"I saw a dog play the piano on TV once," the motor bike man remarked. "He could pick out the keys with his paw. Maybe you could teach this little guy the same thing."

"We don't have a piano," Emmie replied, as the song on the radio ended. Fleabiscuit stopped wagging his tail, and I started wagging my finger. "You're not a greyhound, and you better not run off like that ever again!" Fleabiscuit plopped down on the sidewalk and looked up at me, as if to say he was sorry for taking off. Of course, that's just what I was reading into his eyes, which seemed to have grown bigger, darker, and shinier. I'm not sure dogs know

what apologies are, but if they do, this was one
of them.

"You could buy him a toy piano," the motor
bike man suggested. "He may be one of those musical hounds. He could get famous, you know."

"He's not our dog," Emmie answered. She's
got an answer for everything, whether her head
hurts or not. On the way home, when she wasn't
complaining, she never stopped talking about getting a keyboard and teaching Fleabiscuit to play
melodies with his paws. "Mr. Muffin wouldn't
mind," she said.

It was all I could do to keep from putting my
hand over her mouth. I reminded myself that she
was only seven. In her imagination, dogs could play
the piano in concert halls and for all I knew, cats
could pilot jet airplanes, too.

eight

When Emmie gets even a little sick, it's like the world stops. Grandma begins boiling special tea on the stove and makes the whole place smell like old shoes. Mama stops smiling, and Uncle Travis yells at the fire engines for making too much noise as they drive by. My sister lies on the couch in front of the TV watching reruns. She's the only person I know who loves having a thermometer in her mouth.

As I was heading out the door to pick up Fleabiscuit for our walk, Mama gave me a bunch of last-minute instructions:

"Please, stop at the drugstore on your way back from walking the dog. Here's a list of things to pick up. Be careful crossing the street. Don't lose the money. Don't dawdle. Hurry back."

When I got to Mr. Muffin's place, Fleabiscuit was waiting at the door. He was swinging his rear end and going wild as soon as Mr. Muffin handed me the leash. Suddenly, I got an idea. "May I take him home to visit my sister? She's sick, and I know Fleabiscuit would cheer her up." Mr. Muffin agreed and added,"I'll give you some extra cookies. Maybe they'll make her feel better, too." He said he knew what it was like to feel like a Danish—cheesy. Ha ha.

On the way to the pharmacy, I passed a new pet shop that had puppies hopping around in the window. I figured Fleabiscuit might like looking at some of them, but when I lifted him up, he didn't seem all that interested. Two ladies dressed exactly alike in T-shirts with black dogs on them were standing next to us. When they saw Fleabiscuit, they started asking questions. "Is he a mutt?" the taller lady asked. She got busy scratching Fleabiscuit's head and said, "He's just adorable!"

"He's not a mutt." That came out of me real fast.

"Oh? What breed is he?" the other lady wanted to know.

"He's a Woodlawn Mountain Riff," I said. "A whole-full-complete breed," I added.

"Really? Well, I'm going to go right inside and see if I can order a Mountain Riff puppy!" the tall lady said. She and her friend practically ran into the store.

Right away I figured it was time to go, and I picked up Fleabiscuit and took off. I flew down the street, and when I stopped to wait for a light at the corner, I looked back. The owner of the pet shop was standing in the doorway. He seemed to be looking up and down the street for me, wanting to check out a dog breed that doesn't exist.

I decided to get as far away as fast as I could. I turned a corner I hadn't intended to. I found myself on a street I try to steer clear of: the street where we used to live. Our apartment was right near the corner, in a building made of dark red brick. It had an iron railing that Dad and I painted together the summer before he died. It's the railing that bothers me most; I remember how we put on the orange anti-rust stuff first and then slicked on the black paint with brushes we dipped into big metal cans. I used to feel so good when I saw how we'd turned the iron bars from dull and chipped to shiny and new.

Most of all, I remember having my own room off the kitchen. I had my own radio, too, and could close the door and listen to music and not be disturbed. I even had my own closet, with only my stuff in it, and a big Knicks poster and a fish tank with two goldfish—and my own desk under the window.

I didn't stay very long because it makes me sad, and Mama had said not to dawdle. I quickly turned around and headed to the pharmacy. As I carried Fleabiscuit through the glass doors of the drugstore, a guard inside stopped me. "No dogs allowed in here, sonny," he said, and he held out his arms on either side to block my way. He wasn't giving an inch. "Sorry. You can't bring him in," he said. "Store policy."

I went back outside and looked up and down the street, hoping I'd see someone I knew who would watch Fleabiscuit for a few minutes. For what seemed like forever, I looked for a face that was familiar. Finally a man in a wheelchair rolled toward me. I figured no one in a wheelchair could kidnap a dog, so I stopped him and asked if he would mind very much watching a puppy for just a little while.

The man looked at his watch. "Five minutes is all I've got," he said. He swiveled his wheelchair around and told me he'd hold him on his lap. "What's his name?" he asked.

I introduced Fleabiscuit and thanked the man umpteen times and promised I wouldn't be gone any longer than five minutes.

nine

As it turned out, I was in the drugstore much longer than five minutes. I figured the man in the wheelchair would understand when I explained I had to wait at the checkout. But when I ran out of the store, he was nowhere in sight. Gone!

A lot of skin-crawling thoughts went through my head. Who wouldn't want a supercool puppy with Fleabiscuit's face and personality? Maybe the man had just rolled his wheelchair into a taxi and taken off. He could be in another borough now! Or maybe he'd sold Fleabiscuit to the ladies I'd seen in front of the pet store for a thousand dollars!

The sidewalk was jammed with people. How would I find a policeman in this crowd? I looked in every direction, checked across the street, and then, yes! Two police officers were heading into a police car parked at the curb. As I began to cross two lanes of traffic to get to them, a familiar voice yelled, "Hey, boy!" When I spun around, I saw the man in the wheelchair right behind me. Fleabiscuit was sitting on his lap, looking healthy and happy, and wagging his tail.

The man, on the other hand, looked red in the face. "Did you forget to tell me something about this animal, boy?" he asked. His voice seemed like a ticking bomb. I couldn't imagine what he was talking about until he showed me the big stain on both his knees. "You didn't tell me he's not housebroken! He piddled all over me the minute you left!"

"Oh, no!" I yelled.

Then the man told me how he'd tried to get into the drugstore to find me, but he couldn't get in with a dog. Next he explained how he'd gone up the block looking for someone to give him paper towels so he could clean his pants. His face got redder and redder and his voice went higher and higher. He handed Fleabiscuit back like he was a bomb about to blow up.

Then came the real earth shaker, like it was nothing at all. "Did you say the dog's name was Fleabiscuit? I guess you did. Well, Fleabiscuit is some dog. I never heard a dog sing before."

"Pardon?"

"I said, it's definitely a first for me, hearing a

dog sing notes like that."

"Did you say *sing*?"

"Yeah. You never heard him?"

"I never—"

"He sang, all right!"

"Fleabiscuit *sang*?"

The man nodded. "Vocalized," he said, and then he sang a few notes of the scale—"*La-la-la-la*"—to demonstrate.

I thought that maybe Fleabiscuit's accident messed up something in his head. Dogs can't sing, so I thought I'd better get away from this person. You never know.

"Well, it was right up there, near the corner," the man continued as I was backing away. He pointed in the direction of the traffic light. "The cops had stopped a big white convertible—top down, probably speeding—and the music was coming out of the car radio, loud, very loud—a coupla college boys joyriding, I guess—and all of a sudden, I hear this melody coming out of this little dog here—"

I shook my head. He was exaggerating. Fleabiscuit is one in a million, and there actually may have been a dog trained to play the piano once, but singing—well, it was definitely time to put some distance between me and this gentleman. "Thanks very much," I said. "I'm sorry about your pants—"

I continued to back away.

"And by the way, two ladies wearing shirts with pictures of black dogs stopped me when they saw him sitting on my lap. They're looking to buy one just like him. I didn't realize he was a pure-bred Woodlawn Mountain Riff! That's a rare breed, isn't it?"

ten

Fleabiscuit and I were walking home when
I heard a car behind me beep-beeping its horn. I
turned and saw Roebuck pulling over to the curb. A
minute later, he was rolling down the window of his
silver car and waving me over. "I looked for your
mother today, but she wasn't on her usual corner.
Everything okay?"

"Emmie's sick," I told him, and he scribbled
something on the back of a picture postcard and
handed it to me. "I wrote down my cellphone number. Tell your mother if she needs a ride anywhere
to call me. And tell her I hope your sister's feeling
good soon, okay?"

When I got home, Emmie and Mama weren't there.
The TV was on full blast for Grandma's favorite
soap opera, but she wasn't watching it. She wasn't
sewing either. She was sitting in front of the TV

with her eyes closed tight, but she wasn't sleeping. Uncle Travis told me Emmie's fever had gone up and Mama had taken her to the hospital emergency room. Although it was too early for stars, he was working hard looking at the sky. He was trying to find something up there to pray to, even if it was a cloud shaped like one of the saints. "But all I can see are clouds shaped like bags of laundry," he said.

When Mama and Emmie came home, Emmie wasn't talking, which was not a good sign. She was looking pink around the eyes and just wanted to lie down and go to sleep. Mama also looked pink around the eyes, but *she* couldn't seem to sit still, even when I handed her Roebuck's postcard.

She took the things I'd brought from the drugstore and put them in the bathroom, then gave me a humongous hug. When she finally let me go, she yelled at Grandma to turn down the TV, saying the commercials could be heard all the way across the river. She asked Uncle Travis how come if he spent all his time sitting at the window he always forgot to water the houseplants on the sills? The heat was killing them! Like Grandma, Mama has black-thread days, too, so I tried to cheer her up. I told her to eat a cookie and to hope with every bite that Emmie would get better in a hurry.

That night, Uncle Travis had one of his

dreams. I practically catapulted out of bed when he let out screams that sounded like a fire engine was coming through the room. I switched on the light, and that woke him right up. By the time Mama was in the doorway, he was sitting up and lighting a cigarette. She flew over and grabbed it out of his hand like it was a stick of dynamite.

"Smoking! And in the bedroom! What are you thinking? You're making the air smell like a dump site!" I closed my eyes and thought of our old place. No smoke, no commotion, no Uncle Travis. Just me in my own room. Then I figured Uncle Travis wanted his own place, too. I told myself to remember to get a cookie for him. Maybe we could both hope his dreams would improve and he'd never have to light up a cigarette again.

eleven

When I woke up the next morning, Emmie was standing at the foot of my bed. She had a piece of toast in her hand, jelly all over her mouth, and wanted to know why I was still sleeping. "You're supposed to be sick," I told her. "I was," she said. "Now I'm better."

Even so, Mama would not let her go outside. Otherwise she would have tagged along when I picked up Fleabiscuit for his walk. Of course, as usual, he ran circles of excitement around my feet as soon as he saw me. I would even say he was smiling, but who would believe me? As soon as we got outside, he started to pull me toward the park. He must have been there once, because he seemed to know the way, and he was definitely in a hurry to get to it.

It was Saturday, and Emmie wasn't there to tell me the park was too far, her feet hurt, she was thirsty and needed a drink. So before you knew it, we got there. People were rollerblading, biking, pushing strollers, and holding balloons. Little kids were running all over the place, and a couple of babies were crying. There were hot dog vendors, pretzel and soda guys, and a woman in a clown hat juggling what looked like colored bowling pins. Then, up ahead, I saw a man playing a trumpet. He had a blue rhythm box strapped around his neck that blared like a ten-piece band.

Suddenly Fleabiscuit's second ear, the right one, stood straight up like it wanted to fly off his head. He began tugging at the leash like crazy, pulling me in the direction of the music. The trumpet man had put a black felt hat on the ground in front of him. People were standing in a circle, throwing change into it. The man kept right on playing, and the music seemed to be everywhere. It was like there were speakers hidden in the benches, buried under his feet, or hanging in the trees above his head.

The trumpet man had closed his eyes and was playing with all his heart, and if a dog can be said to be listening with all *his* heart, that would tell you how Fleabiscuit looked. With both ears standing up stiff as shirt cardboard, he moved his head first to one side, then to the other, a look of doggy joy locked on his fuzzy face.

Next, the musician began playing a song that was sort of slow and had a lot of high notes and then some low ones—a foreign song I've never heard before. That's when Fleabiscuit let out a little excited bark and jumped up on his hind legs like one of those trick poodles in the circus. That lasted only a second; Fleabiscuit's legs were obviously made to work best as a foursome. He wiggled his body, wagged his tail, and suddenly let out a sound I had never in my whole life heard come out of a dog before.

It wasn't exactly a wail or a cry. It wasn't a bark or a warble. It was something you'd hear in the studio of an opera singer who was practicing or a sound you might hear coming from the mouth of a voice teacher giving a lesson. It went high, it went low, it was—and you couldn't call it anything else—*singing*.

It was *amazing*!

I'm not saying Fleabiscuit was good at carrying a tune, and I'm not saying he belonged on the stage of the Metropolitan Opera House. I'm saying that when the trumpet man played his slow number, Fleabiscuit sang along, off-key maybe, missing some notes for sure, but his chin was up, his eyes were closed, and a real melody was coming out of his shaggy little mouth.

One by one, the people standing around in the circle began to notice. How could they not? Fleabiscuit's voice was loud and getting louder. First, there were giggles, then a commotion started: "Hey! A singing dog!" someone cried, and the circle got bigger. People were pointing, laughing, and trying to get a better look. The trumpet man kept playing, but his eyes were wide open now, looking as if they might come popping right out of his head.

And Fleabiscuit sang on.

twelve

When I took Fleabiscuit back to Mr. Muffin, he noticed that both ears were sticking up. I told him about what happened in the park, and he just threw back his head and laughed. "If Fleabiscuit was that musical, he should have been named Éclair de Lune, everyone's favorite piano melody," he said. It was obvious he didn't believe much of what I'd told him. When he gave me a cookie, I decided not to say that I thought one of them had helped my sister get better. His Hope cookies were like fourleaf clovers, wishing wells, and the number 9. He'd probably laugh if I mentioned those, too.

Luckily, when I told Mama what had happened at the park, she believed me. Well, sort of.

"Sometimes dogs make sounds like woofy wails or barking cries that sound like singing," she said.

"No, Mama, Fleabiscuit *sang*," I assured her, but just then Mama began sniffing the air and making a face.

"I think Travis is smoking again! Dropping ashes right into my plants!"

And Grandma piped up that no new orders had come in in weeks and said, "The world is going to pot in more ways than one if people aren't putting initials on things anymore!"

Then Mama told Emmie and me that we were going to the cemetery. She warned Travis that if the air wasn't smoke-free by the time we got back, he'd be in for it. "And I mean you'll be in big-time, whopping trouble!" she added.

I always sit by the window on the way to the cemetery on the bus, and Emmie sits by the window on the way back. That's how come I was looking out but not really looking out until I saw the dog on a leash. A kid not much older than Emmie was walking him along the sidewalk. I practically jumped out of my seat. The bus had stopped to let on some passengers, so I had a minute to really look. The dog was a duplicate of Fleabiscuit! It had the same face and the same short little legs and shaggy body. Both ears were flopped down like Fleabiscuit's when I first laid eyes on him. He was not *exactly*

Fleabiscuit-like, though. The expression on his face was just not as *swank*. Not as *sharp*. I could tell that although this dog looked the same, could even be a twin, he didn't have Fleabiscuit's personality.

On the other hand, I was knocked for a loop. Maybe Fleabiscuit had a brother or sister. Maybe two or three! "Look at that dog!" I cried, pointing out the window. "Where, where?" Emmie leaned over me, smelling like the grape lollipop that stuck out of her mouth and made her teeth and lips a ghoulish purple. "What, what?"

"A dog that looks just like Fleabiscuit," I said. "You missed it," I told her as the bus took off.

"No, no I didn't!" she said. "I saw it! I did! It looked just like Fleabiscuit. It was so *droll!*"

It was the only time that whole day that Mama smiled.

I don't like going to the cemetery. I hate looking at the grass that covers the spot where Daddy is lying forever asleep. I don't like seeing Mama's face when she puts flowers next to the headstone, either. Today, though, with Fleabiscuit on my mind every minute, I imagined that Daddy's spirit was with me. And I was sure it was smiling.

When I went to pick up Fleabiscuit at Mr. Muffin's

later that day, I was surprised that his granddaughter opened the door. "You don't have to walk the puppy today," she said. "I'm staying overnight. I'm afraid Grandpa isn't feeling well."

I heard Mr. Muffin's voice calling out from the back of the apartment. "I'm feeling crummy but I'll be fine tomorrow. Come back then! And give the kid a cookie anyway; we got more than enough," he directed his granddaughter.

Fleabiscuit was dancing around my feet as usual. I was plenty disappointed not to get him to myself for an hour or two. I'd wanted to take him to our apartment so Mama could sing to him. Maybe he would join in the way he had at the park yesterday.

Mr. Muffin's granddaughter told me her grandfather was wearing himself out baking every day. "From now on he'll give you a dollar instead, all right?"

Anyone else would have been okay with that, but I'd come to count on Mr. Muffin's cookies, and not just for their taste. As I walked upstairs to our apartment taking small bites, I hoped he'd feel well enough to keep up his good work. I had lots of hopes, wishes, and desires all lined up and waiting to go.

thirteen

School started. An e-mail from Ziggy came for me on my media room computer, Emmie lost two bottom teeth, and the school nurse said I grew two inches. I got a look at my new math teacher — who looked like she could breathe fire—and my new English teacher. He said, "I give more homework than anybody," and he meant it. The first night I was into forty pages of *The Day Lincoln Was Shot* when the doorbell buzzed. It was Mr. Muffin's granddaughter and Fleabiscuit.

"I'm taking my grandfather to the doctor's. Could you walk the puppy today?"

The family, all of us, were at home, so it was my chance to show everyone, even Mr. Muffin's granddaughter, what Fleabiscuit could do. After I told her what had happened at the park, she had agreed to stick around for the demonstration as long as it didn't last more than a few minutes. Grandma turned off the TV, Uncle Travis left the window, Emmie got quiet for once in her life, and Mama offered Mr. Muffin's granddaughter a glass of iced tea. Then Mama turned on the tape deck and put on one of her own tapes. We sat in a sort of circle, all eyes on Fleabiscuit. Right away I saw his head go left and right, east and west, the way it does whenever he hears music. I could see the way his doggy self was absorbing every note, and I thought for sure his vocal cords were getting ready for action.

But although he opened his mouth to yawn, he didn't sing. He didn't bark or cry or wail or anything. With everyone sitting around, every eye on him, he just sat there on the little rug in the center of the room and listened. He was so quiet, you would have thought he was in the public library. Of course, Mama tried another tape. And another and another. Fleabiscuit never moved. He seemed to love being here, must have thought it was a concert just for him. But he never let out a single peep. Instead, Grandma got into another sneezing fit—obviously, she's allergic to dogs—and had to step outside for some fresh air.

I decided I'd try to play something myself. Maybe one of the songs I'd practiced would inspire Fleabiscuit. I pulled my xylophone out of the hall closet and began "La Bamba," which I know real well. I do such a great job with that number that once, when I was playing it at the Fourteenth Street subway stop, a man started whistling, clapping, and dancing, and he got so jazzed up he almost fell off the platform onto the tracks.

Fleabiscuit stood up, wagged his tail, and for a minute I thought *This is it!* But—he plopped right down again. Keeping both eyes on me—everyone said he kept them on me every minute—not a sound came out of him!

Of course, I was embarrassed. Who wouldn't be? Mama knew I wouldn't make anything up, but Mr. Muffin's granddaughter might have thought I'd imagined the whole thing. Emmie started chatting away: "I bet Fleabiscuit just has a sore throat. Maybe he needs his tonsils out." Uncle Travis called it puppy stage fright, and Grandma asked, "Did the dog sing? I didn't hear him sing!"

Mama said she herself was very disappointed. Then she offered another glass of iced tea to Mr. Muffin's granddaughter, who said she shouldn't have stayed so long, it was getting very late and her grandfather was waiting. "Fleabiscuit may not be Elvis Presley, but Grandpa loves him just the same," she said to me, her eyes getting a little teary. I wasn't sure why she was so sad. I figured it was because she'd had her hopes up, Fleabiscuit had let everyone down, and she was disappointed too. And maybe it was also that Mr. Muffin wasn't feeling so good. When Mama put an arm around her shoulders, I figured that's what it really was.

I took Fleabiscuit for a long walk right after I finished my homework. When we stopped at a corner to wait for the light, I tried talking to him. "What happened to you today?" I asked, trying not to sound annoyed. Of course, I didn't really expect an answer. Did I imagine what I'd seen in the park had never happened? Not for a minute. I'd heard Fleabiscuit sing once, and I figured, sooner or later, I'd hear him sing again.

Grandma knew I was disappointed, and I guess that's why she made chocolate pudding for dessert that night. When I'd finished eating half of mine, Uncle Travis let out a sort of whoop. "Hey! Look out there!" he yelled. His voice was so loud I almost dropped my spoon.

"You'll never believe it!" he said, waving us all over to take a look. Emmie and I dropped everything, of course, and ran to the window.

"Look over there—" Uncle Travis was pointing toward the corner at the newspaper and magazine store. "Look at those two dogs! They're exactly like Fleabiscuit! They don't have the black spot, but otherwise, they could be his baby brothers!"

"Or sisters!" Emmie said.

He was right. The dogs looked like a pair of Fleabiscuit's relatives. But what really surprised me was who was holding the leashes. I was sure it was one of the two ladies I'd seen looking into the window of the pet store a few weeks ago. They had been wearing Black Dog T-shirts then, but now they were in matching plaid shirts and jeans.

"Aren't you going to finish your pudding?" Grandma asked when I jumped up from the table.

"What's he doing? Where's he going? Can I go too?" Emmie asked as I ran out the door and flew down the stairs.

I caught up with the ladies halfway up the next block. Of course, I had a lot of questions to ask. I knew where Mr. Muffin's granddaughter had found Fleabiscuit—at the dog and cat shelter—but where had another two just like him come from?

"Excuse me," I said, out of breath from running. "I'm wondering, could your dogs and Fleabiscuit be, like, cousins or something?"

The ladies remembered me, and they were very friendly. "Oh, I don't think they're relatives," one said.

I got up my nerve to ask the most important question. "Did you by any chance ever hear them *sing?*" That's really why I'd chased after them, leaving my chocolate pudding on the table where Emmie could get at it.

"Sing? *Sing?*" The ladies looked at each other and rolled their eyes. "We can't even get them paper-trained!" the taller lady said.

I told them I'd heard Fleabiscuit carry a melody with my own two ears.

"Send us the CD when he records one," the shorter lady said. They had a big laugh over that. Then, as I turned to go back home and was feeling pretty disappointed, the shorter lady called out, "You told us your dog was a Woodlawn Mountain Riff, didn't you?" She was wearing eyeglasses with big frames and looked as if she'd love every book on my new English teacher's reading list. "You were very wrong. We found these puppies at a kennel in Connecticut, and they are not Riffs. They are genuine Glen of Imaal Terriers."

The taller lady was nodding a mile a minute. "They are purebred Irish dogs," she said. "*Working* dogs. They have a long history of herding sheep." The shorter lady agreed. "We got on the Internet and went through a lot of pictures. That's how we found these darlings," she said. "As for Woodlawn Mountain Riffs, I believe they are yellow short-haired dogs with long tails. Isn't that right?"

fourteen

I charged up to Mr. Muffin's the very next day after school. When he opened the door, he said he was feeling pretty stale but was glad to see me. I blurted out, "Did you know Fleabiscuit was a Glen of Imaal Terrier, an Irish dog?"

"If I'd known, I'da got him a green collar," Mr. Muffin said. "Anyway, he's from the pound up on 110th Street, not from Dublin," he added.

I know German Shepherds aren't all from Germany and Scotties aren't all from Scotland, but I didn't want to argue.

"May I take him back to our house for just a little while? I want my mom to sing to him again."

"Why? You think you're gonna get another ear to come up out of his head?" Mr. Muffin let out a laugh mixed with a couple of coughs.

"Just a half hour, okay?" I asked, and I was

out the door before he could think of another funny answer.

I got back to our place just as Mama was about to leave to take Emmie to have her teeth cleaned. She was in a hurry, but I begged and pleaded.

"He's an Irish dog, Mama. Maybe he only knows Irish music."

"No time now. We have to go to the dentist's, then be at the Thirty-fourth Street subway stop at 4:30!" Mama said. She was still not convinced that what we had here was a dog who could make history.

"Just one song, Mama!"

"Irish music is not really my specialty, Nicky."

"Please, just sing 'Danny Boy' once. *Once!*"

Emmie was only too happy to put off dental work, and she began to do what she does best. She begged and pleaded. "Sing 'Danny Boy,' just a few notes, please, Mama," until Mama finally gave in. She got Grandma to turn down the TV. I wanted Uncle Travis here for this occasion, but he was taking a nap. Mama wouldn't let me wake him. "He was up half the night at the window. He has to sleep sometime," she said.

I got Fleabiscuit to stop running around and wagging hello to everyone. Finally, he sat down on the couch next to me and everyone grew quiet.

Mama stood in the middle of the room and began to sing "Danny Boy" a cappella. *A cappella* means without accompaniment. I would have been glad to get out my xylophone and join in, but I don't know how to play that song. And although Emmie knows how to play five flute solos—sort of—that is just not one of them.

But never mind! Mama began very softly, "Oh, Danny Boy, the pipes, the pipes are calling . . ." Right away, I saw Fleabiscuit come to attention, his head going back and forth as always, and his black-olive eyes sparkling like they were behind glass. He began to wag his tail a little, and then he put his chin up in the air, opened his mouth, and let out some notes that were not wails, not howls, and they were definitely not cries. They were a doggy version of "Danny Boy." He did not exactly have perfect pitch, but he sang loud and clear, practically drowning out Mama's voice.

I saw Mama's eyes go wide then, not just ordinary wide, but round, dark and huge. It was a *big moment.*

Emmie, who was sitting on the other side of Fleabiscuit, let out a little shriek of surprise, and Uncle Travis appeared in the doorway rubbing his eyes. I watched his mouth open and then stay there in amazement. Mama continued to sing and so did

Fleabiscuit, his head up, his little rose-pink tongue vibrating as he sang. His eyes were shut, as if he were really concentrating, as if this song, at this minute, meant just about everything in his little Irish doggy life.

And then Grandma's eyes got very red and she began to sneeze, one *kerchoo* after another, and the concert was over.

fifteen

It turned out that Fleabiscuit sang whenever he heard "Danny Boy" or "Galway Bay" or "An Irish Lullaby," but he didn't know "When Irish Eyes Are Smiling" or "McNamara's Band" or any of the other Irish songs Mama could think of. We also found out he'd been left at the shelter by a musician who had to go back to Kilkenny or Kildare or someplace in Ireland and had no one to look after his puppy here in New York City. We didn't find that out until later, when Mr. Muffin's granddaughter checked the records at the kennel where she'd adopted him.

We got permission from Mr. Muffin to take Fleabiscuit to his very first subway recital. First, though, we rehearsed those three songs with him like a hundred times. We had to go up on the roof so Grandma wouldn't get into a sneezing fit. She said she'd always been allergic to cats, but a dog allergy was something that must have come on recently. She guessed it was because of the "close living quarters." I was sure she wanted her apartment to herself again as much as we wanted one of our own.

I taught myself Fleabiscuit's songs by listening to a tape Mama made for me. Emmie got help with her flute from a music teacher in school, but she still had trouble with "Galway Bay" and the lullaby. She did get "Danny Boy" down pat—well, almost—and on the next Wednesday, a week and a half after we'd first heard Fleabiscuit sing, we got ready to head to the Thirty-fourth Street subway stop.

Mama got Emmie some kind of yellow skirt and Grandma embroidered it all over with what looked like bumblebees. And, of course, Emmie put on her favorite winking, blinking shoes. She was so excited she talked double time.

"*Shhh*, Emmie, *shhhhhh*," Mama kept saying, but off Emmie went, faster and louder than ever. She talked about how people would pour out of every train to hear us perform, and we'd stop subway traffic every time Fleabiscuit opened his mouth.

"We'll get rich as kings. Soon we'll be living on top of a mountain in a castle with a swimming pool with a slide," she said, and whatever other stream of thought popped into her head.

As we were about to leave, Grandma called

after us. She had a surprise. She'd made a little coat out of an old denim shirt of Uncle Travis's. On one side, she'd embroidered FLEABISCUIT. On the other, THE SINGING DOG, all in bright green thread. She'd even stitched a little four-leaf clover on top for good luck. I wished I had a Hope cookie, since I didn't believe as much in four-leaf clovers, but Mr. Muffin hadn't been up to baking for some time.

As soon as I put the jacket on Fleabiscuit, Emmie cried, "Oh, look at him, doesn't he look *enchanting?*" another of her Internet vocabulary words. That got Mama to come up with one of her big, melodious smiles, the first one I'd seen in a long while. Uncle Travis took a picture of all of us before we headed out the door.

"This is one dog who knows how to smile for the camera," he said. We had such high hopes that we were practically singing and dancing all the way down the stairs.

We carried Fleabiscuit in our straw money basket when we took the subway to Thirty-fourth Street. I didn't want anyone stepping on one of his paws, which were still no bigger than quarters. Emmie told him we'd get there very soon. "Only three more stops," she'd say, or "We're already at Fifty-ninth Street," or "Almost there!" She kept him posted, as if he could understand. He stuck his face out of the top of the basket and kept licking her hand, as if he actually understood what she was saying. More proof Fleabiscuit was going to be a headliner!

Finally, we arrived at Thirty-fourth Street and waited at our assigned spot under the black and orange MUSIC UNDER NEW YORK banner. As Mama set up her tape player and I took my xylophone out of its carrying case and we got Fleabiscuit out of his basket, I admit I was plenty nervous.

Suppose the crowds scared him? Suppose he made a puddle right here? Even Emmie had gotten quiet. She took off her jacket and pulled at her yellow bumblebee skirt and made sure her shoelaces were tied. I got out my mallets and told myself Fleabiscuit would not let us down. Mama looked at me and gave me a wink.

"Ready?" she said.

I nodded and Emmie picked up her flute and put it to her mouth. People were rushing by, hardly giving us a glance even as I tied Fleabiscuit's leash to the leg of my xylophone. I gave him a word of encouragement. "You're about to become a star," I whispered. Mama turned on the tape player and picked up the little black microphone she always uses.

She was going to let Fleabiscuit sing the

melody after she sang the introduction, but all she managed to get out were three bars. It's always the unexpected that messes everything up. Sure enough, before Fleabiscuit had even opened his mouth, before Emmie had blown a note on her flute and before my mallet had hit even one key of my xylophone, two policemen arrived!

sixteen

The two policemen looked like giants in uniforms, and the expression on their faces was strictly law-and-order. Guns were hanging from their belts, next to very scary black clubs. As they came closer, I spotted handcuffs, too, shiny and dangerous, ready for action.

Mama leaned over and turned off the tape machine, Emmie looked as if she'd already been handcuffed—ghost-white and terrified—and I nearly dropped my mallets.

One policeman faced Mama and pointed to Fleabiscuit. "Is that a dog?" he asked.

What sort of question was that? Was he trying to be funny? What else could Fleabiscuit be? Mama nodded, and I could see she didn't know how to answer.

"Is that a Seeing Eye dog?" the policeman asked now.

Mama shook her head no.

"Lady, you know better, don't you? Only Seeing Eye dogs are allowed in the subway!"

"I didn't know," Mama said, and one of the policeman's eyebrows went up. I could tell he didn't really believe her.

"Well, now you know," he said, and he waved his arm at the big EXIT sign at the end of the platform. "You've got to get the canine out of here." He wasn't being mean or anything, but he definitely meant business.

"We were about to let him sing—," Mama tried to explain. "He's not just a dog. He's a performer."

The second policeman looked amused when she said that. "Oh, a singing dog. Right," he said. "A baritone? A bass? What?" The two policemen gave each other look-what-we-have-to-deal-with looks. They thought it was very funny.

"If you just let us play a little bit—," Mama answered. "You'll hear for yourselves."

"No dogs. It's the law."

"You could just listen for five minutes—"

"If you don't get the animal out of here right now, I'll have to impound it and give you a summons, ma'am." The policeman's voice was polite but it had a punch. I hoped Mama wouldn't argue anymore. It's not good to stand under a tree during a thunderstorm, not smart to dive off a pier into the Hudson River, and it's asking for trouble to argue with the police; things everybody knows! A few people were beginning to gather, wondering what law we'd broken and probably waiting to see us get arrested. Emmie leaned against Mama, looking as if she'd crash to the floor if Mama moved an inch.

"I'm only asking for five—"

"Ma'am!" The second policeman took a step toward Fleabiscuit and gave the leash a little tug. Fleabiscuit looked up; I think he was very surprised. "I don't want to hear any more about this. Pavarotti goes. *Now.*" The policeman's eyebrows had moved together into one dark and angry stripe.

"Mama, please, let's go," I said. My mother looked at me for a long, awful minute and finally she nodded. She picked up her tape machine and told Emmie to put her flute back in its case.

When the policemen saw that we were going to leave without any more arguments, the taller one leaned over and patted Fleabiscuit on the head. "He's a cute little fella," he said. Then he added, "Sorry, folks, but even if he's the reincarnation of Frank Sinatra, you gotta understand, the law is the law."

On the way up the escalator, Mama reached

over and smoothed Emmie's hair. My sister was crying so hard strangers were staring, assuming we'd done some awful thing to the poor child. You could see it on their faces; everyone was sorry for her. To my surprise, I was, too.

seventeen

"If he can't sing in the subway, no reason he can't sing in the park," I suggested to Mama. I'd watched the crowds gather the day Fleabiscuit did his first solo with the trumpet player. He'd drawn a crowd, and I remembered the piles of change and bills in the trumpet player's hat.

"Why not, why not, why not?" Emmie chimed in. I'd brought Fleabiscuit back to Mr. Muffin and told him about the policemen. "They have *some* crust!" he said, then added, "but for the most part, they're there when you need them and they're pretty good eggs." He offered me a slice of berry pie. Because he hadn't felt like baking in a while, his granddaughter had made the pie for him, and he hoped I'd take home what was left for my family. "My granddaughter did not inherit my baking gene," he said, giving me a wink. "It's a good pie, a decent piece of work, but not world-class. Not a *Hope* pie, if you know what I mean." As I kissed Fleabiscuit good-bye for the day, Mr. Muffin reassured me, "It'll all work out for the best. You'll see."

I wasn't so sure because the park idea had fizzled. Now that it was getting colder outside, Mama was working at a thrift store on Saturdays. On Sundays we went to church and then out to the cemetery. During the week, when Emmie and I got home from school, there were never enough people in the park to make a concert worthwhile. And there was always English homework: umpteen pages to read. Besides, the leaves were beginning to fall and soon it would be too cold. People would not stand and listen to music when their toes were freezing in their shoes.

It was dark gloom in our apartment for days and days. Uncle Travis sat at the window most of the day and half the night as usual, sneaking cigarettes. Grandma was sewing initials and flowers onto a pile of linen handkerchiefs, a small order from a department store, and then complaining that no more orders had come in. The TV was louder than ever, and Emmie was following me around every minute or pleading with Mama to buy her a set of little china dishes or a new jacket with a fake fur collar or socks with lace around the edges, whatever she'd seen on TV or on some kid in her class. She took the picture Uncle Travis had taken of all of us—Fleabiscuit in his new coat, Mama all smiles—and tacked it on the wall over the dresser she shares with Grandma in their room.

I kept walking Fleabiscuit after school but nowadays Mr. Muffin sometimes forgot to slip me a dollar. I'd go up on the roof once in a while and play one of Fleabiscuit's three Irish songs. He'd join in and sing every time. I tried to teach him "Santa Lucia." He'd listen and look at me as if to say, "I hear it and I'm thinking it over," but not a sound came out of him. Maybe, I thought, he was just waiting for the right moment.

By this time I could take Fleabiscuit off his leash and he'd stay right next to me. He was housebroken one hundred percent, but I noticed when I dropped him off after we'd spent an afternoon together, he'd look really let down. His head would hang, his tail would droop, and there'd be a little slump in his shaggy shoulders. He'd go right to his bed in the corner and curl up, looking up at me as if to say, "Where do you think you're going without me?" On the other hand, when I arrived at Mr. Muffin's apartment, not only did he dart around in crazy circles but he'd jump so high into the air, he was like a trick dog.

Meantime, Mama, Emmie, and I kept doing our singing and playing at the subway stops at Fourteenth Street, Seventy-second Street, and in Greenwich Village at Astor Place. Although we added two or three new numbers and made a bunch of new tapes, we never sold more than four or five in one session, no matter how hard I tried.

Then, a few weeks later, Uncle Travis woke me up in the middle of the night. He shook me so hard, I thought he'd had one of his bad dreams. Because he was so excited, I imagined there was a fire; for a second I thought I even smelled smoke. I shot up in bed. "Get up, get up! Come look out the window!" he yelled. I raced over to see what mind-bending, chilling thing was out there. A white ambulance with flashing red lights was parked at the curb under our windows. PRESBYTERIAN HOSPITAL was written on its side.

A bed on wheels was being rolled into it. Someone wrapped in white sheets was lying on the bed, and two men all in white were closing the ambulance's back doors. "You know who that is, don't you?" Uncle Travis said.

He'd opened the window and I was shivering like crazy. "Not Mr. Muffin!" I couldn't stop shaking.

Uncle Travis put his arm around my shoulder. "It's Mr. Muffin, all right," he said. "And it doesn't look good, does it?"

eighteen

Even though I'd almost gotten through
The Day Lincoln Was Shot and finished my math
homework, I didn't want to go to school the next
day. Was Fleabiscuit up in Mr. Muffin's apartment
alone? What would become of him? Both Mama
and Grandma were very upset. They were worried
about Mr. Muffin and said an ambulance in front of
the building also reminded them of the day Daddy
went to the hospital. But, no matter what, I
couldn't stay home. They promised that while I was
at school, they would keep an eye out for Mr.
Muffin's granddaughter.

Sure enough, when I came running home at
three o'clock, Mama handed me a letter. Mr.
Muffin's granddaughter had brought Fleabiscuit to
our place, hoping we could look after him. But
when Mama explained about Grandma's allergy, she
wrote me a letter, folded it, and put my name on it.

Dear Nicky:
While Grandpa is in the hospital, I will
try to take care of Fleabiscuit. If you
want to come visit him, here is my
address:
341 Grinnell Street
Sleepy Hollow, New York
I know he will miss you very much, so try
to come if you can.

I added up the house number in my head.
Three and four and one equaled eight, not a lucky 9
as I'd hoped. "Where's Sleepy Hollow?" I asked. It
sounded far away, but then and there I decided no
matter how far, I'd go—until Mama told me the bad
news. It wasn't a place I could get to on
Rollerblades, a scooter, a bus, or a subway. It was a
village on the Hudson River, a long train ride away.
The biggest problem was the fare. It cost about as
much as a new jacket at the thrift shop: too much.

That same afternoon, Mama and Emmie and I
had to perform at the subway stop at Union Square.
It was one of our best assignments because it's such
a busy station, but my heart wasn't in it. We did
"Proud Mary," which I'd learned, and some of the
Beatles songs everyone loves. Emmie went around
with the basket. When we were in the middle of

"Let It Be," a man in a leather jacket who must have missed about three trains just to stand and listen to us, asked Mama if she'd sing "Michelle." He said it was his daughter's name and his favorite song. Mama sang the song so beautifully that a few minutes later, the man came over and gave her a red rose. Then he decided to buy one of our tapes, and, out of the blue, I got a little memory-bolt.

When he opened his leather jacket to reach into his pocket to get some money, I noticed his shirt. It was patterned with swirls and dots and leaves like you'd find in a florist's place or on birthday gift-wrapping paper. It reminded me of the shirt Roebuck had worn the first time I'd seen him. Roebuck! It was like someone had yanked a cord, pulling up a shade in my head. "If you ever need a ride," he'd said, handing me his cellphone number on a picture postcard. I'd forgotten all about it.

But where had I put that card?

I remembered! I'd given it to Mama. And then *she* remembered taking it. But she couldn't recall what she'd done with it. "I put it in my pocket and I guess I never bothered to take it out," she said. She was sorry she'd been too busy to give it much thought. "I put it in the pocket of a jacket I was wearing that day," she said. "Just give me a little bit of time to think about where that jacket might be.

It's probably hanging in my closet."

But later, when she looked for it, she realized she no longer had it. "It's in the pocket of one of the things I gave to the thrift shop at the end of the season," she said. "It was a very old, faded blue jacket that Grandma had embroidered with a little white horse with wings, just like the one on Dad's Road Runner cap." She ran over to give me an I'm-sorry hug, but I didn't really feel like a hug just then.

I wanted to *give* one. I wanted to go to Sleepy Hollow, wherever that was, and have Fleabiscuit run circles around my legs and pick him up and give *him* one.

I felt terrible. It was as if I were being punished and hadn't done anything wrong. I guess it was my turn to have some black-thread days, a whole, awful bunch of them.

nineteen

A few days later we were singing at the Thirty-fourth Street station. Just as Mama was finishing "Stand by Me," a man with a gray beard, a polka-dot bow tie, and a nice suit like you'd see in church, came walking over to our basket with a dollar in his hand. I noticed his shoelaces were each a different color, and he had a big smile on his face.

"Fine job," he said, giving Mama a thumbs-up, and he saluted Emmie, who was about to take a bow. "What kind of xylophone is that?" he asked me when the song ended. I told him it was a Piccolo Kelon. He seemed very interested, touching the keyboard and examining the mallets. Next thing I knew, he leaned down, grabbed our basket, and ran off and up the subway stairs faster than an Olympic sprinter. He'd taken all the money we'd collected that afternoon.

"Stop!" I yelled, dropping my mallets. I raced

after him, as Mama yelled after me to come back. She was afraid he might have a gun or a hand grenade or who knows what, but I just kept going like my legs were on automatic speed-pilot. I flew up the stairs and yelled, "*Stop! Stop! Stop!*" louder and louder, and "*Thief! Thief! Thief!*" with my voice cracking and splitting like the sound effects in a battle video.

Two policemen came out of nowhere. They were definitely "the good eggs" Mr. Muffin had said would be there when I needed them. They'd heard me yell and believe it or not, they caught him! They grabbed the thief by both shoulders and made him kneel right there on the sidewalk. "Is this yours?" one policeman asked me, holding out the basket, which the dressed-up crook had smushed under his arm. It was an amazing moment, because right behind me was another man, wearing a dark blue hooded sweatshirt. He was perspiring and very excited, pointing at the thief, who was being handcuffed. "That's the guy who stole my wallet!" he said when he saw the dressed-up crook with his hands behind his back, his face red, and his chin hanging so low it was covering his bow tie and part of his shirt. "He just reached into my back pocket and swiped it when I was about to get on the train!"

All I'd done was run after the man, but the policemen gave me full credit for the arrest. "If this boy hadn't chased him, he'd have gotten clean away with it." One policeman put a hand on my shoulder, and the man in the hooded sweatshirt pulled a ten-dollar bill out of the wallet the other policeman had returned to him. He told me he was very grateful. "You are a brave youngster and a credit to the community." I felt like I'd just grown a foot.

But I hesitated before accepting the money. Should I take it? Mama would have said no, but by the time she came huffing and puffing up the stairs looking for me with Emmie crying right behind her, I had the bill tucked into *my* back pocket. A crowd had gathered, and I felt all eyes were on me. People were saying I had courage and nerve and that I was daring. I must admit I was feeling very, very proud of myself. "Stop crying, I'm okay," I told my sister, who was embarrassing me by hanging on to my sleeve with both hands. Judging by the tears dripping off her face and chin, she must have thought she and Mama would find me flat dead on the sidewalk.

I patted my back pocket. Ten dollars! It was folded up small, just waiting to be spent! I began to think I actually deserved it. While the police were getting ready to take the thief to the police station, I made a decision. I had the money; I'd go to Sleepy Hollow this very minute.

It seemed best to keep the plan to myself. I knew Mama wouldn't let me go alone. She might also make me spend the ten dollars on something practical, something at the thrift store. I knew she'd find a pair of handcuffs and lock me up in a safe place if she thought I was even thinking of getting on a train out of the city by myself.

"I'll be home later," I told her, but I didn't give her a chance to ask any questions about where I was headed. The policemen both shook my hand and wished me good luck, and I took off before Mama could stop me. A few long crosstown blocks and eight short ones didn't add up to a lucky 9, but I ran like the wind. Fleabiscuit was waiting for me. The thief had done me a big favor, or so I thought. "Here I come, Fleabiscuit!" I was saying to myself. I could practically see him jumping up and giving my face a licky kiss and almost hear him singing "Danny Boy" until the music in my head changed. That happened a few minutes later—at the ticket window in Grand Central station.

twenty

Grand Central station is very big, full of halls with shops and restaurants, stairs and wide doorways leading to tunnels and train tracks. It took me longer than I expected to find the ticket windows. Then I had to wait in a long line. There were lots of people behind me, waiting their turns. Other people were rushing past in every direction, carrying briefcases and newspapers, luggage and shopping bags, running for trains. I wondered how I'd ever find the right train myself. The lady behind the ticket window smiled at me. "Where would you like to go?" she asked.

"Sleepy Hollow," I told her.

"Do you want a single fare or a round-trip ticket?" she asked. What a question! I had to come back, didn't I? As it was, I knew Mama would be boiling mad and worried if I wasn't home by suppertime.

"A round-trip," I said, which is when the lady

asked how old I was. "Twelve," I answered, and telling the truth turned out to get me very bad news.

"That will be a full adult fare: thirteen dollars and thirty cents."

If I'd said I was eleven-and-a-half, I would have been on my way! "I've only been twelve for a few months," I told the ticket lady.

She shrugged, her smile did a fade-out and she asked me to step aside. "People will miss their trains if they can't buy their tickets. You're holding up the line."

I moved off, not knowing what to do next. Above the ticket office I could see a huge sign listing all the trains and where they were going. Feeling shot down, I thought the closest I'd get to Sleepy Hollow today—and maybe ever—was reading the name of the town on that sign. The train I should take was leaving in fifteen minutes, on track 125. Of course, I noticed that the one and the two and the five did not add up to nine. I thought that if I just went to that track, some lucky thing, some Grand Central miracle, would get me on that train bound for Fleabiscuit.

I looked left, I looked right, but 125 did not seem to be anywhere in sight. Then I noticed a man with a pair of gray and white mop-like dogs on leashes. He was crossing the terminal, a backpack on his back and the dogs pulling ahead. Maybe if I explained about how important it was for me to get to Sleepy Hollow, how really *urgent*, he'd understand. He would know how it would feel if his dogs moved far away, how he'd miss them every minute, how he'd wake up thinking about them and fall asleep worrying about whether he'd ever get to see them again. I raced over just as the man was about to walk through the gate to the platform where his train was waiting. "Excuse me," I said. He stopped and listened politely as I explained about Fleabiscuit. It all poured out of me in a rush: how I only had ten dollars, how Fleabiscuit must be very homesick, how all I needed was three little dollars and thirty cents, how I'd pay it back and that that was a rock-solid promise. . .

"*Je ne parle pas Anglais.*" The man cut me off with a shrug and a look of apology. In English, he added, "Sorry," and gave me little wave that was sort of a salute. Then he walked down the platform, put one little dog after the other into a carrying case and stepped onto the train.

When I finally found track 125—it was down a flight of stairs on the lower level of the station—I saw the train to Sleepy Hollow. It was just sitting there, waiting to go without me. I felt about as black-thread grim as I'd felt all year. People jostled by in a hurry to get on board, and there were no miracles in sight. I thought of jumping onto the last car, hopping on as the train left the station like an animated character in a cartoon movie. But that was against the law, not to mention dangerous.

So I just hung around there for the longest time, looking at the back of the train. I watched the conductors standing at the open doors and thought of asking one of them if I could possibly hitch a ride on credit, owe the railroad the extra money, but I didn't have the nerve. I kept imagining Fleabiscuit, sitting at a window somewhere up there in faraway Sleepy Hollow, sad as anything, wondering where I was, just waiting for me to come for him.

While I stood watching, still hoping for some unexpected last-minute miracle, the train pulled out of the station. That's when I sank down, right onto the cold stone floor on the lower level of Grand Central station. It was just too hard to stand up for even one more minute. I didn't want to walk or wait or try to think of some other way to get to see Fleabiscuit again. I just folded up like a marionette in front of the gate of track 125 like my arms, legs, and especially my feet, had stopped working.

And then I heard music. It was coming from behind me. It was loud, too, and live. Funny thing is, it happened to be "La Bamba." I thought of "La

Bamba" as *our* song, which I know it isn't, but I'd been playing it again and again. It was Emmie's favorite; she dances up a storm even if I just do the first chorus. So I got up from the stone floor kind of slowly to see where the music was coming from. And there, at the foot of the stairs leading up to the main terminal, was a man playing a saxophone, another playing guitar, and a third with a keyboard. Above them was the black and orange banner: MUSIC UNDER NEW YORK.

Of course, I stopped to listen. A crowd had gathered. More people were standing in a circle, tapping their feet, swaying with the music, and smiling. There were men and women and kids, too, and even a blind man with his Seeing Eye dog. And there was a girl a little older than Emmie who was selling tapes, distributing them left and right, making change and handing out both CDs and cassettes. And people were buying them like crazy.

The ten dollar bill was still folded in my pocket. I touched it to make sure it was there. I needed some of it to get home. I had to talk to Mama in a hurry. Life came back into my feet. I wanted her to come and see for herself what we could do in a place like this, where there were bunches and batches and crowds of people everywhere you looked, a place just made for us to play and sing in—a huge and busy place that not only allowed, but would probably welcome and celebrate, a singing dog.

I ran, I flew, I practically skimmed through the air to get home, full of hope and pumped up like a jet. I'd failed today, but there was always tomorrow. I *had* to get to Sleepy Hollow. I'd carry Fleabiscuit in our money basket just like the man who'd carried his dogs onto the train.

I'd take Fleabiscuit to Grand Central station to let the world hear him sing.

twenty one

"And *THEN* what?" Mama said. She was so mad at me her face was red all the way down her neck. As soon as I walked in the door, she grabbed me by the shoulders and gave me a shake. "Look! Will you please look outside!" she said. I know I am not allowed to be out after dark, but wasn't this crisis an exception? Mama didn't think so.

She yelled at me for about ten minutes after I explained. What was I thinking to go off like that without telling her? Had I gone crazy to imagine she'd ever let me get on a train to go anywhere alone? How was I planning to find Fleabiscuit once I got up there? And this next point made her face even redder—if I'd actually found him and brought him back to the city, then what? Where would the poor puppy sleep? Not here! And Mr. Muffin was still in the hospital and might not be back for weeks!

Emmie said she'd been afraid I'd fallen into a

manhole, and Uncle Travis just threw up his hands. He guessed I'd gotten a thousand-dollar reward and thought I'd been out there with my money on a spending spree, stuffing my face with candy and black cherry soda—his favorite. Or maybe, he'd said, some bad electricity had got me too.

Even Grandma chimed in, saying she'd been praying all afternoon that no bad people had kidnapped me. Mama wouldn't listen to a word I was telling her about Grand Central station and our chance at making music history.

Now came the punishment.

"You're not to leave the apartment except to play in our scheduled performances! And to go to school! And to go with me to the supermarket!" With those few "Ands," Mama was putting a lid on my life, and that was only the half of it.

"And since you'll be spending a whole bunch of time at home, you can keep busy cleaning out closets and maybe washing a few windows!" When her face gets this red and when her voice goes this high, there is no arguing with Mama. I looked at my plate of dinner and couldn't eat a thing.

The next day after school, Mama took what was left of my ten dollars and dragged me to the thrift shop. She made me try on blue jackets and brown ones, pushed up the collars and checked out the lapels. Every time I tried on another coat, she said the sleeves were too short or the shoulders were too big, or she touched the material and said it wouldn't keep me warm enough. She made me stand in front of a mirror with three parts and looked at three of me from the front and the back and the sides.

Finally, she found a jacket she thought was just right. It was gray with silver buttons and suede patches at the elbows. She asked me what I thought of it. What could I say? I hardly saw myself in the mirror at all. It was as if my soul had left my body.

"It's okay, I guess," I said.

On the way home, Mama stopped at the supermarket. She had a list and sent me to the freezer department for some things we needed while she went to look for salad stuff. While I was searching for frozen blueberries, I looked up and there it was, smack in front of my eyes: Mama's old faded blue jacket, the one with the flying horse Grandma had embroidered on the front. It was the one she was wearing when I gave her the card with Roebuck's cellphone number on it.

A teenage girl with her hair dyed blue was wearing it. There was no mistake—it was my mother's old jacket. The girl had about twenty silver bracelets on her wrist that were clinking as she pulled juice out of the freezer. Her basket was filled with cat food.

"Excuse me," I said, and she squinted suspicious rays at me. I could see the jacket was kind of big on her. "I believe that's my mother's jacket," I said.

Right away the girl shook her head no, and a sort of get-lost look came across her face. "I mean, it used to be," I explained, and quickly asked if she'd search through the pockets because there was probably a very important telephone number in one of them. "Could you please look?" I asked her. Of course, a lot of thoughts came whirling through my head. Roebuck would definitely be glad to drive us all to Sleepy Hollow!

"There's nothing in any of the pockets except a little bit of change, some lint, and my sunglasses," the girl said, and she pulled out a pair of glasses with blue lenses to show me. "Anyway, it's not my jacket. It's my mother's," she added. "I just borrowed it."

When I found Mama, she was putting radishes into her grocery basket. "Your jacket! It's here!" I told her.

"Leave it to you, Nicky!" she said, and she asked if I'd found the frozen blueberries. Sometimes I don't understand my mother. While I'm thinking

96

life and death and making music history, she's thinking waffles and pancakes.

"We have to find Roebuck," I told her, and she must have noticed the look on my face, because she dropped the lettuce she'd just picked up and reached into her pocketbook to pull out a pen and a piece of paper.

twenty two

The girl wrote down her address for me
after I begged and pleaded and told her it was about
a missing puppy. Then Mama wouldn't let me go to
the place alone. She waited on the sidewalk while I
rang the bell. It was a gray building on a corner, next
to a Chinese laundry with steamed-up windows.

I must have rung the bell three times before
the door finally opened. A lady with those big
curlers that look like pink plumbing supplies talked
to me over a chain, asking me what I wanted. She
looked as if she thought I might break in, throw all
her silverware into a pillowcase, and take off with it.
I guess I look honest enough, because after I
explained about the postcard Mama had left in her
jacket, she let me in.

When I explained for the second or third time
why I needed to find the card, a funny smile came
over this lady's face. It was as if she had a surprise

she was about to spring on me.

"Follow me," she said, and she led the way through a hallway that had pictures of cats all over the walls, and then into a bedroom.

In the middle of the room was a bed with two cats lying on the pillows, one white and one every color a cat could be all mixed in together, both looking up at me as if to say, "What are you doing here?"

"They're my sweet babies," the lady said, then told me she understood exactly how I felt about Fleabiscuit. "I had a dog who died at age nineteen the night before Christmas two years ago."

Her eyes got teary, and then she pointed to a table that had twenty or thirty little bottles of lotions and potions all over it. I tried to figure out where exactly she was pointing, but all I saw were more photographs of cats, a few of her now dead dog and some of babies, flowers, and saints. There were some regular people, too, and all were stuck around this mirror.

And then, there it was! The card that Roebuck had given me with his phone number on the back. I recognized it right away—a bunch of sheep standing in front of a building with a big, half-broken door and a flag with a white star in the middle right next to it.

"That's San Antonio, Texas. My sister lives

there. When I found the picture-postcard in the pocket of the jacket, I couldn't throw it away. It's beautiful! Maybe you'll go to San Antonio someday and see for yourself!"

Even the cats on the bed now looked as if they were smiling at me. I could have hugged the lady, I was so happy. I told her I definitely hoped I'd go there soon and thanked her a thousand times. Then I ran out into the street to show Mama the card with Roebuck's name and cellphone number written in black ink, clear as anything, right on the back of it.

twenty three

"He's here!" Uncle Travis said, and I flew over to the window. Sure enough, Roebuck's silver car was waiting right outside. Mama said it looked like Roebuck had put it through the car wash, but Uncle Travis said it was more likely that he'd polished it to within an inch of its life, just to impress Mama. He added, "And just look at the way he's standing at the curb, gazing up at our windows! Like he's seeing the aurora borealis or something."

Mama and I waved at Roebuck and called, "We'll be right down!" In the meantime, Emmie kept bopping around, asking if she could sit in the front seat and fussing with the barrettes in her hair. A few minutes after that, I caught her in the bathroom about to spray herself with Mama's perfume. "You'd think you'd never been in a car before," Grandma said. The truth was, she had only been in yellow cabs, mostly when she was sick and had to go to the doctor's. And this was no yellow cab. This was fancy, it was sleek, it was almost a limousine!

As soon as we got downstairs, I looked through the car windows and saw that the seats were dark blue and sort of like velvet. "Not even a speck of lint!" Mama whispered as we climbed in. Emmie didn't get to sit up front, and neither did I. It was Mama who got to sit next to Roebuck. He said she deserved to sit in the seat of honor. It was after she'd presented him with a little surprise gift. Grandma had embroidered a handkerchief with his initials: R.S., which stood for Roebuck Sears. "We didn't know your middle name," Mama explained. Roebuck told us it was O'Malley. "My mother was Irish," he added, and Mama said if she'd known that, she'd have asked Grandma to use green thread and add the same four-leaf clover she'd put on Fleabiscuit's coat. Then she told him that Fleabiscuit only knows Irish songs. When Roebuck asked, "Would he know 'When Irish Eyes Are Smiling'? It's my favorite," there was a tap on the car window next to Mama.

It was Mr. Muffin's granddaughter. We almost didn't recognize her. She'd cut her hair and put on a pair of eyeglasses. Her face didn't look all smiles and friendly as usual. I knew right away she had something to tell us, and it wasn't going to be good.

"Grandpa is leaving the hospital," she said, when Mama finally got the window down, "but he's not coming home. He's going into a nursing home."

My mouth opened and closed, the name "Fleabiscuit" with a question mark on the tip of my tongue, but no sound came out. Emmie was bobbing up and down in her seat. "If Mr. Muffin is going to a nursing home, will they give him milk in bottles with rubber nipples on top?" she whispered.

Mama was asking Mr. Muffin's granddaughter questions, too, about his health and where the nursing home was. "Will he be there for long?" she wanted to know. From his granddaughter's answers, I learned that his pacemaker had not kept up the rhythm of his heartbeat well enough.

"Grandpa will be better off in a place where people will take good care of him, instead of up in his apartment alone," she said.

Then Mr. Muffin's granddaughter looked over my mother's shoulder right at me. She must have guessed what was on my mind. "I know you'll be sorry to hear this," she said, and stopped for a second, sort of getting her voice under cruise control. "I have a new job and couldn't take care of Fleabiscuit any longer."

She took off her glasses and rubbed her fingers

across her eyelids. Roebuck passed his new handkerchief to Mama, and Mama passed it to Mr. Muffin's granddaughter. She wiped her eyes with it, and Emmie whispered, "She's *crying*!" After she'd handed back the handkerchief, she told us she'd taken Fleabiscuit to the animal shelter. "It's where I got him," she explained. She rushed on, looking like she was going to need a handkerchief again. "Someone good will certainly adopt Fleabiscuit and give him a wonderful home. I don't want you to worry."

It was like I'd been thrown into a lifeboat in the middle of the ocean and someone had just torpedoed a hole in its side.

Emmie sort of erupted. "You mean we're never going to see him again?" she cried, looking like she was going to burst into tears herself.

There was a crashing wave of silence, like Emmie hadn't even been heard. Of course, it was my question, too, and no one would answer it. I imagined Fleabiscuit sitting at the door of a strange house in a strange city, sad as anything, just waiting for me to come for him. For all I knew, he'd curl up in a corner and never get up again.

Now Mr. Muffin's granddaughter was digging into her purse for something. Finally, she found it. "I almost forgot. Grandpa wanted you to have this," she said. She stuck her hand through the window and gave me a yellow envelope. "He's never given it to anyone else, ever. He told me to tell you not to make the oven too hot and always to hope for the best. It's the recipe. You know, for the Hope cookies."

twenty four

Roebuck said he'd drive us to Coney Island to cheer us up. Emmie and I were pretty quiet in the backseat, and when we got there, I couldn't get even one bite of hot dog down. It goes to show you how *not* important fancy cars can be if the scenery in your head doesn't have a bit of sunshine anywhere in it.

All I could think about was getting Fleabiscuit out of the shelter. That's when I got the idea of baking the Hope cookies.

I knew Mama didn't have time, and I figured Grandma would get too busy monogramming all our towels to bake. So what I did next was a little extreme. I went to bed like I was supposed to, but made myself stay awake. I waited until everyone else was asleep—even Uncle Travis—and then got up and tiptoed into the kitchen. How hard could it be to follow Mr. Muffin's recipe? Grandma had pinned it on the refrigerator door with a magnet. I took it down and began to read:

Preheat oven to 350 degrees.

I examined the knobs, dials, and buttons, opened the oven door and stared into it. Then I took a deep breath, pushed a knob, pulled out a button, and turned a dial. A red light went on. Easy!

I checked out the recipe. *Smush together the first five ingredients until you have a ball of dough.* It sounded like fun! I kept reading. It was roll this, add that, cut this, mix that. If I could just follow these directions, I'd have the cookies made, one-two-three.

I pulled equipment out of the drawers and from over the sink. I took out the butter and found vanilla, white chocolate bits, butterscotch bits, and two kinds of sugar. I climbed to the high cupboard where Grandma keeps the flour, spilling only a little on the way down.

I was pretty sure this was going to be a smooth ride. The cookies would be ready by the time everybody got up for breakfast. Grandma would be thanking me for saving her a job. I might have managed it, too, if it wasn't for Uncle Travis. I was trying to figure out how to "grease a cookie tin" when he had one of his bad dreams and let out a couple of screams that shook the walls. I froze right there, with a cookie tin in one hand and a bar of squishy butter in the other. Sure enough, the noise woke Mama. Before I knew it, she was standing in the doorway of the kitchen.

"What do you think you're doing!" Her eyes were jumping around from floor to stove to refrigerator to me. For a second I thought the ceiling might come raining down in a storm of plaster.

I looked around. The kitchen was a mess. The cabinets were hanging open. In addition to the flour I spilled, some confectioner's sugar had fallen on the floor with a bit of butter and eggshells and other stuff. There was flour on the cabinet doors where my fingers had left marks.

I don't remember all of what Mama said. Uncle Travis was standing in the doorway, totally recovered from his dream. Then Grandma came in, her hair bunched up from sleeping, and the three of them wedged in between the stove and the table.

Uncle Travis said, "I guess baking cookies is no piece of cake, ha ha," but no one else laughed. Grandma let out a noise, like a minor-key chord played on an electric guitar. Her eyes almost closed as she tried to take it all in without her glasses. That's when the real disaster hit.

Grandma took a step toward me and slipped on something I had dripped on the floor. Before we could catch her, down she went.

Luckily, Emmie slept through it all.

twenty five

As it turned out, Grandma's bones didn't break, but it was bad enough. Grandma had twisted her ankle. The next day, she lay on the couch, her foot resting on a pile of pillows. It stuck out of her slipper, puffed out and pink, and looked pretty sick. Uncle Travis was in charge of changing the ice in her ice bag and bringing her aspirin. When I got home from school, I was in charge of making sandwiches for dinner. I put extra tuna fish on Grandma's tuna melt and extra ice cream on her pie to show her I was really, really sorry.

"It's *dire*," Emmie kept saying, and that's exactly what it was.

All week long, I kept thinking of Fleabiscuit alone in the dog pound. I looked up the address of the shelter. It was on 110th Street and First Avenue. Finally, on Saturday afternoon, after my haircut, taking out the trash, and helping Uncle Travis at the

Laundromat, I got my chance. Mama had gone someplace with Emmie, and both Grandma and Uncle Travis were taking naps.

I ran almost all the way to First Avenue. Anybody seeing me speed along would have thought I was practicing for the Olympics. When I finally reached 110th Street, I stopped cold, frozen to the sidewalk.

The animal shelter was made of stone, the kind that might have been used for pyramids or mausoleums, a sort of gray-white rock meant to last for seventeen lifetimes. It looked like a fortress without a moat, a place with rock-hard walls, a place no kid would ever dare to enter, and there I stood, afraid to go inside. But not for long. I took a deep breath and stepped through the doors.

The first thing that hit me was the smell. *Wow*! It was a major animal kingdom-zoo-circus odor. I'd stepped into a waiting room with a little desk on one side and a big desk on the other. Pictures of dogs and cats hung next to some green double doors. A lady at the little desk smiled at me and directed me to the other side of the room, where two more ladies were waiting to hear what I'd come for. I wasn't even sure. If I rescued Fleabiscuit, where would I take him? I decided to worry about that later as another lady walked in from the back.

She was holding a big, wrinkled looking dog wearing a heavy leather collar.

"I'm here about a dog," I began. "His name is Fleabiscuit, and I want to adopt him."

The ladies looked at each other and then at me. One of them had earrings all in a row up and down her ear.

"You'll have to bring your mother or father with you, son," she said. "We don't allow minors to adopt animals." She kept smiling, but I had the feeling she was a rules person; I was a minor, and that was that. The lady holding the wrinkly dog moved off to answer a telephone.

"But he's actually almost mine anyway," I said, jumping in, ready to explain everything, ready to spend the next hour and a half telling them how Fleabiscuit had landed here in dog jail and I had come to get him out.

The lady with the row of earrings kept smiling. Then she said "It's policy. An adult has to come in here with you."

"If I can't adopt him, may I just go inside and visit him?" I asked.

"Unless someone's adopting, we don't allow them to walk through the kennels. It upsets the animals," she said, upsetting *me*.

"Just for a minute?" I pleaded. "If I could just

talk to him for a minute, just say hello—" The lady shook her head and wouldn't budge. I tried to tell her that Fleabiscuit was a remarkable dog, a singing phenomenon, but she cut me off. A man carrying a baby had come in. He was looking for a lost cat. She went to the computer behind the desk and started fiddling with the keyboard.

Now is my chance! I thought. I quietly eased my way toward the green double doors. I could get to them in about four very quiet, quick steps while the lady was busy looking at the computer screen. Fleabiscuit would be behind them somewhere, and overjoyed to see me, for sure!

I moved so quietly you would have thought I was a jewel thief. Sure enough, in four quick steps I was at the green doors. I didn't look left or right, just put my hand on the first doorknob and pulled hard. I tried the second.

Of course, I should have known it: The green doors—both of them—were locked tight.

twenty six

It wasn't the first time of course, but right now I missed Dad like crazy. I needed him to help me, tell me what to do. While I stood there thinking, the baby spotted the wrinkled-up dog held by one of the ladies behind the desk, and for some reason, started screaming his little head off. There was a terrific commotion. The dog jumped out of the lady's arms and made a big mistake on the floor about an inch from the earring lady's shoe.

Almost right away the green double doors opened. A tall man with a mop and bucket stepped out. While he was concentrating on the baby screams and the wrinkly-dog mess, I slipped through the doors before they closed.

Then I was undercover in a hallway. On the wall were pictures of every species of animal you could imagine—including a snake—but no living

animal in sight. Instead, there were doors, one
after another, all closed, leading to who-knows
where. I tried the first one and stepped into a
room of cages, one stacked on top of another. In
each one there was either a cat or a kitten or two
kittens together. There were fuzzy ones and thin
ones, black ones and sleepy ones, every single
one looking at me with green or yellow eyes,
wanting me to let them out. Maybe that was just
my imagination, but I backed out of that room in
a hurry, feeling I'd let all of them down.

I tried the next door. Dogs! I got very excited. I rushed from cage to cage—these were
stacked, too—and I came face-to-face with some
big and some not-so-big, leggy or lumpy, furry
or sleek, scared or ferocious, all different speci-
mens, none of them Fleabiscuit. After I backed
out of this room, I tried the next door. More
dogs. I ran from cage to cage; there were so
many! Some were just puppies that could hardly
stand on their own little wobbly legs. I began to
worry; there were so many dogs here, what if I
couldn't find Fleabiscuit? A few were starting to
bark now; any minute one of the ladies could
come in here to see what the problem was and
find me. Maybe I'd be arrested before I could
find Fleabiscuit! "Fleabiscuit!" I began calling.

"Fleabiscuit! Fleabiscuit!" More barking, yelping, and howling. The noise!

Then, out of nowhere, an idea zoomed into my head. I opened my mouth and started to sing. My voice creaked and cracked, but I got out a few bars of "Danny Boy" as loud as I could. "Oh, Danny Boy, the pipes, the pipes are caaaaalllling. . . . My voice went into overdrive. It snapped and split, went up, went down, but then—

Fleabiscuit answered. I heard his voice as clear as anything, right through the barks and howls. He was singing!

It took only a minute or two to find him. He was in a cage between two other cages. One held a pop-eyed dog scratching his head, the other a little mouse of a dog scrunched in a corner, looking scared to death. And there was Fleabiscuit, his nose pushing against the metal cage, his tail wagging, his paws up, scratching at the bars, his eyes so big and wet I was sure he'd spent every minute of his time here crying them out.

"I'll try to get you out, one way or another," I told him. His head tilted left and right and left again when I spoke. I stuck my fingers into his cage, and he licked my thumb. Why hadn't I thought to bring a dog biscuit? Or *something*? It hurt to think he'd see me turn around and walk right out without him. I reached down and took off my shoe, pulled off one of my socks, and stuck it into the little cage. He'd have a little memento of me, at least for now. "I will try everything to get you out," I whispered again, swallowing hard, and thinking, *But how will I?*

And then I got caught.

"What are you doing in here?" the tall man with the mop asked.

I didn't answer. I needed a tissue. "You're not allowed in here, sonny, you know that," he said, but I could tell he wasn't mean. He leaned over to look into my face and his voice went really soft. With all the barks and howls, I could barely hear him. "Don't worry, boy, most of these little fellas will be adopted sooner or later. The cats, too. They're in good hands here."

He put his hand on my shoulder and walked me out. "Your little guy will be okay, too. Now you go home, it's getting dark. Don't worry about these puppies. We take real good care of them. We love them all."

When I got home Mama wanted to know what happened to my right sock. I didn't want to tell her. She asked me three times, and finally, Emmie asked if my foot wasn't cold. I told her no, and she said I was obviously *slipshod* about my feet. Everyone laughed at that, even Mama, who thinks Emmie's showing off new, weird words is cute. Everyone, that is, except me.

twenty seven

The next day after church, Roebuck drove
Mama and Emmie to the cemetery. I told Mama I
had extra homework and that was true. It was also
true my homework was to convince Uncle Travis to
go to the animal shelter with me. With him along,
I'd get Fleabiscuit out of that cage in a hurry.

Uncle Travis was in no rush to go all the
way to 110th Street, especially today. Although
Grandma's ankle was much better, he said she'd
been cooped up too long. He wanted to take her out
for some fresh air. Then he planned to take a nap,
clip his fingernails, and read the last chapter of an
astronomy book he hadn't finished. All in all,
"Today is not a good day," he informed me.

He also asked where I intended to take
Fleabiscuit, how I would feed him, where we'd
sleep. "It's all just pie in the sky, y'know," he said,
sounding a lot like Mr. Muffin.

"I'll take him to Grand Central station," I explained. "He'll sing and we'll make enough money to move to a new place." I wasn't exactly sure how this was going to work, but I'd figure it out somehow.

"Uncle Travis, you've got to help me get Fleabiscuit out of the pound!"

"Maybe I'll go there with you one day next week," he said. Uncle Travis was in the bathroom shaving. All I wanted was to push him down the stairs and out the door. We could be at the shelter in half an hour.

I added, "Fleabiscuit will make so much money singing we'll be able to buy you a telescope."

That did it. A smile spread across Uncle Travis's face. "Okay, we'll go there, why not? Soon as I get back from taking your grandma for a walk, okay?"

It was pretty late by the time we got started, but I relaxed. We were finally on our way. Once Uncle Travis stopped to buy some cigarettes, making me promise not to tell. He also stopped at a few stores and newsstands to look at some magazines. He liked to check out the latest in cosmology and astrophysics. "Things are changing in the sky every day," he said, flipping magazine pages a mile a minute while I waited and waited, practically jumping up and down with impatience.

When we got to the shelter, the lady with the row of earrings who had been behind the desk was gone. A guy in a New York Mets sweatshirt had taken her place. He was wearing only one earring. He put down his water bottle and gave us a big hello. "And what may I do for you fine folks today?"

"We've come to adopt a dog, his name is Fleabiscuit, he's in there—" I said, pointing to the green doors. "He's waiting for me to come get him. This is my uncle and he's a grown-up so—"

The guy behind the counter held up a hand to stop me. "Let me look him up," he said, and he picked up a pair of glasses and slipped them over his ears. "Fleabiscuit? Okay, do you happen to know the breed?"

I almost said he was a Woodlawn Mountain Riff, but stopped myself just in time. "He's a Glen of Imaal Terrier," I told him. I think my voice went gliding along three octaves in about ten seconds.

The man behind the desk squinted through his glasses at the computer screen. After a few minutes, he said, "Fleabiscuit. Right. Glen of Imaal Terrier. Check. Well, there you go. It's right here on my screen. He's been adopted."

I opened my mouth to speak but nothing came

out. Then "But I was here just yesterday!" burst out of me.

Uncle Travis had his hand on my elbow. I guess he was making sure I wouldn't slide to the floor like Grandma.

"Adopted this morning. Sorry about that."

"By whom?" I squawked.

"Take it easy, Nicky," my uncle said.

"Sorry, we're not allowed to give out that information." The guy took off his glasses, leaned over, and looked at me. "But there's no reason to be disappointed. We have hundreds of other pooches here to choose from. Kittens, too." When he saw my face, he shrugged. "Well, think about it, folks. We're open seven days a week. You can come back anytime."

twenty eight

Uncle Travis tried to cheer me up. He said Fleabiscuit would be better off in a good home. Maybe his new family owned a place in the country with a big backyard and a good view of the sky. Then he changed his approach and said he'd help me find the new owner and try to get Fleabiscuit back. Finally, he said I'd find him within a day or two; after all, a singing dog wouldn't be that hard to locate!

I didn't say a word the whole way home. The blackest thoughts were jammed together in my head. Maybe Fleabiscuit was happy with his new owner, but what about me? I wasn't going to have much of a life without him. I knew right then and there that it wasn't about his singing, either. It was about *him*. He and I were of a different species. I couldn't always read his thoughts any more than he could understand every word I said, but there was something awesome between us. We really did understand each other. We both knew he was supposed to be *my* dog.

When we got to our front step, Uncle Travis gave me a long, hard look. "He was sort of a special pooch, so I can't blame you for being sad," he said. Then he apologized for selling my watch. He pulled a big handkerchief out of his pocket, monogrammed in blue by Grandma, and handed it to me. I guess he could see I needed to blow my nose.

As soon as we stepped through the door, I knew something was different. It was the smell. It was an odor I recognized immediately, and it was perfume to my nose.

"They'll be ready in a minute," Grandma said. "Hope cookies!"

I walked into the kitchen and stood in front of the oven door waiting for the timer to go off. When it did, I let out a yell. It was as loud as my voice could go. "They're ready!"

Grandma made me wait until they cooled, but pretty soon, I was eating one, and then another. "You'll spoil your dinner," she warned when I reached for a third. Her stew was bubbling on the stove, but a bigger stew was bubbling right in my head.

Now that I'd eaten a couple of cookies, I was filled top to bottom with hope. But in the city of

New York, where there are a zillion people, how would I ever find one fuzzy little dog?

About four hours later Emmie came into my room.

"So. What are you doing?" she asked me.

"Homework, as if you didn't know," I said, pointing to the door. "Can't talk now."

But it was like she didn't hear me. She began asking me a thousand questions, starting with what was it like to see all those dogs in their cages at the shelter.

"Did you cry when you heard that Fleabiscuit was adopted?"

"No. Of course not," I said.

"Uncle Travis said you did. He said it right after you left dinner to go do your homework."

"He's wrong. I was just sniffling because I'm getting a cold."

Then a look came over her face that made me not order her out of the room. Some little know-it-all sparkle under her smart-alecky eyebrows stopped me from pulling her physically off my bed and pushing her out the door.

"Is something on your mind?" I asked her.

"Maybe."

"You know something I don't."

"It's a possibility."

"Could you please stop showing off words?"

She made a face and crossed her arms across her T-shirt.

"What is it then?"

"I can't tell. It's a secret."

I know my sister well enough to know she'll keep a hair ribbon or a marble in her drawer for the rest of her life, but she can't keep a secret for more than fifteen minutes. I had to work on her for all of five, threatening her with everything from not taking her to the playground to hiding her light-up shoes in a place where she'd never find them again.

"I know who adopted Fleabiscuit," she finally said. At first, I thought she was making it up. "They weren't going to tell you until your birthday."

My birthday was two and a half weeks away.

"If they find out I told, I'll get in big trouble," she added.

"Oh, no you won't! Definitely not!" I said, assuring her I'd never tell on her. "C'mon, Emmie! I'm your favorite brother!" Uncle Travis's little joke didn't cut it.

"You're my *only* brother."

"Who adopted Fleabiscuit?" I pushed.

She held out for one more minute. By now I could feel my face turning colors.

"Who?" I bellowed.

"You have to promise not to say I told."

"I promise!"

"Roebuck went to the shelter this morning and adopted him. Fleabiscuit's gonna ride in the silver car with him. And Roebuck's going to bring him over for a visit on your birthday."

twenty nine

I told myself two and a half weeks was not so long to wait. Still, each day I looked up and down every street for Roebuck, even checking out the spot in front of the restaurant where I'd first seen him.

Then one night, he came for dinner! As soon as he walked into our living room, I ran downstairs, pretending I'd left one of my school books at the library. Every parking space on the street was filled, so it took me a while to find his car. He'd left it in front of a church around the corner, and when I spotted it shining like a spaceship under a street-light, I had to stop a minute just to catch my breath. Then, I rushed over to look through the windows, front and back. All I saw was a folded newspaper on the front seat and an umbrella in the back. I looked again to make sure. There was something yellow under the newspaper. Could that be the cushion where Fleabiscuit sat, right next to the driver's seat, next to Roebuck?

I guess I was relieved Roebuck hadn't left him sitting in the cold, dark car while he was at our house having dinner. But then, where was Fleabiscuit? At Roebuck's house? In a warm cozy place, having his own puppy-chow dinner? My head was spinning; it was only five more days until my birthday, but I wasn't sure I could last. I spent all dinner struggling not to ask about him, not even to mention Fleabiscuit's name.

Finally, it was my birthday! That morning Mama made me blueberry pancakes and put a marshmallow in my cup of cocoa. Everyone wished me a happy birthday, and I went off to school like every other day. But, I couldn't wait to get home. I was sure Fleabiscuit would be waiting for me when I got there.

Instead, at dinner Uncle Travis presented me with a photograph of the new set of mallets he promised to buy as soon as he had "the proper funds." Grandma handed me a package that had a pair of pajamas with *Nicky* stitched over the pocket. Emmie had made me a birthday card in school that had sparkles all over it that stuck to my fingers. Mama had a big birthday cake waiting for me. Next to it was a wrapped present—which turned out to be a little CD player—and a brown envelope. Something about the way she was looking at me, with one of her melodious smiles, got me thinking she was going to spring Fleabiscuit on me in some new, fun way.

I kept looking at the door, even as I was tearing open the big, brown envelope. I felt everyone's eyes on me when I looked at what was inside: two more envelopes. "Open the white one first," Mama said, and when I did, there was a picture of a bridge. "What is this?" I asked.

"It's the view!" Mama said. "The view from the window of your new room!"

"What new room?" I wanted to know. There was one other picture in the white envelope: a photograph of a big redbrick building with a little circle around one of the windows. "That's the building we're going to be moving to, and that," Mama said, pointing to the circle, "is going to be the window of your own new, private room!" I was speechless.

"Now open the blue envelope," Mama said, looking all excited, and of course, I did. Uncle Travis walked to the TV and turned it off. A bunch of pictures of dogs fell out of the second envelope.

"Roebuck took all those snapshots at the shelter. He paid the adoption fee, and now all you have to do is to go down there and pick out a puppy. It's his birthday present to you."

I found my voice, although it came out as a squeak.

"Where's Fleabiscuit?" I asked. What was my mother thinking of? I was not interested in even looking at any of these other puppies. "I thought Roebuck had adopted him! I thought he was bringing him over today!"

Emmie dropped one of the candles she was pulling out of the cake. "You weren't supposed to know!" she yelled. "You said you wouldn't say anything!"

"Roebuck did adopt him," Mama, said, ignoring Emmie. "That's how come we're getting this apartment. He sold him to one of his rich clients and gave me the check. The client is in the music business, and he's going to take Fleabiscuit on a singing tour around the world."

"Around the world? No!" I cried.

Mama heard me but it didn't seem to register. She went right on. "With what I've saved, Daddy's insurance, a little bank loan and that check, we finally have enough money to move into a nice new place of our own. You'll have your own room! Isn't that what you've always wanted?"

The blueberry pancakes and the birthday cake

all backed up inside me. While Grandma was wiping icing off Emmie's chin, Uncle Travis stood frozen in the middle of pouring himself a glass of milk, and Mama's smile disappeared from her face like a windshield wiper had swished across it. I went to the bathroom and threw cold water at my face. It was all I could do to keep my birthday cake down.

thirty

I know Mama was upset with me. And with my sister, too. I heard her yelling, "I'll never tell you a secret again, Emmie!" But I was having a meltdown. I wouldn't eat what was good for me, wouldn't let Emmie tag along with me, and wouldn't play the xylophone. At school, my hands, feet, and body were there, but my head was absent. I started sitting next to kids who were coughing or sneezing or just looking like they were coming down with something. I was hoping to get sick so that I'd have to go to bed. I'd make Mama feel so sorry for me she'd figure out how to get Fleabiscuit back. Couldn't she see every bit of music had gone out of me?

I finally came down with a cold, and I made the most of it. Even though Mama let me stay home for a few days, she kept saying I'd get over Fleabiscuit as soon as we moved and got a new puppy. Then *she* caught my cold and had to go to bed herself.

But something good came out of that cold: Roebuck caught it. He'd been giving Mama so many rides it was no surprise. Not that I wanted to make Roebuck sick; he was always helping Emmie with her homework and bringing us stuff like bags of jelly beans. He brought me a Buck Howdy CD and a pair of new socks. It's just that when I thought of Roebuck, I thought of his millionaire friend buying Fleabiscuit. Thinking of that was like having a bad dream in the middle of the morning, the afternoon, or even when I was brushing my teeth.

When Roebuck caught the flu, he called Mama and said he felt too awful to come over for dinner on Saturday. He was all aches and coughs and could barely talk. His voice was beginning to sound like mine. As soon as Mama hung up, the phone rang again. It was Roebuck calling back to ask a big favor. He wanted Uncle Travis to drive one of his clients to the airport. Roebuck was feeling too sick to go himself.

"I don't think so. I'm used to buses," Uncle Travis said, but Mama stood in the doorway and stared at him for about five minutes until he backed down. "Just this once," he said, although he knew he couldn't wear Dad's cap on the job—Roebuck's rules.

When Uncle Travis came back from driving

Roebuck's client to the airport, he was all smiles. He brought Mama a bunch of flowers and said driving a silver car was easier than getting a bus through traffic. "Like a spin through the galaxy." He also patted his pocket. "The lady gave me a good tip, too," he said with a wink. He told Roebuck he'd be happy to do it again. Next time, he promised he'd bring Grandma flowers, too, and would save enough to buy me new mallets and take Emmie to an amusement park. Then, while Mama's and my cold got better, Roebuck's got worse. Now my uncle was so busy driving, he had no time to sit at the window and check out the street or look up at the sky.

The following Sunday at breakfast, Uncle Travis announced he was going to pick up Roebuck's rich client at his millionaire's town house and drive *him* to the airport.

"What's his name?" Mama asked.

"Roebuck calls him DoReMi. 'Do' is for money, 'Re' is for records—he makes them—and 'Mi' is for the millions he's got. He is on his way to Europe for a tour—and taking Fleabiscuit with him! Uncle Travis's eyes looked at me uneasily after he threw out this thunderbolt.

"No!" I cried, and everyone stopped eating to look at me. Emmie's eyes practically sprang out of their sockets. I jumped up from my chair and cried, "He can't do that!" all the time knowing he could, and there was nothing in the world I could do about it.

I begged Uncle Travis to take me with him. "I'm your favorite nephew," I reminded him. I pleaded, my voice cracking in three places. I slid to the floor in front of the door and sat there, holding my arms out so Uncle Travis couldn't leave without me. I said my heart was going double time and wouldn't slow down until he allowed me to go with him. Finally, he agreed I could sit in the front seat if I promised not to make trouble.

Mama followed up with more dos and don'ts about being polite and not getting my hopes up, but it was hard to focus.

I ate a healthy breakfast and gave Grandma a kiss. I told Mama I loved her and promised to show Emmie a card trick and to practice a bunch of new songs when I got back. And before I left, I ran into the kitchen and pulled out the plastic box where Grandma stored the Hope cookies. Then I ate a bunch as fast as I could chew and swallow them. I was actually on my way. One way or another, I was going to see Fleabiscuit in just about an hour and a half!

thirty one

Uncle Travis called, "Ready to go, Nicky?"
and I got up, got my coat, and with my stomach
sloshing and gurgling, followed him out the door.

We drove downtown through a lot of traffic,
got stuck behind trucks once or twice, got cut off by
a few taxicabs, almost went through a red light, and
finally reached DoReMi's house. Uncle Travis called
it a brownstone, but it was actually a rocky, dark
gray. It had an iron railing in front of it a lot like the
one we had at our old house. Right away I noticed
the number on the door, 333, and what that added
up to.

"Stay in the car and don't move," Uncle Travis
directed. He'd parked the car next to a fire hydrant,
which is against the law, but it was the closest space
to the house. There would be a lot of luggage to
carry, so he wanted to be as near the front door as
possible. If a policeman came, I was to tell him we'd

be out of there right away and beg him not to give us a parking ticket.

No policemen came; I sat alone in the car for only about two minutes when the front door opened and DoReMi appeared with my uncle right behind him. Uncle Travis carried out a couple of big suitcases, then a couple of small ones, and finally a sort of hanging bag, while DoReMi watched. He was wearing a leather jacket with a fur collar and a dark brown hat with a big brim, and for a second, he turned and disappeared back through his front door. When he came out again, he was carrying a plastic case with a little door at the top and a screened window on either side. It had two handles and a sign that read, KENNEL. A tag was attached to one of the handles. I couldn't read all that was written on it, but when he got closer, I could read, *Dog fed and watered at 2 p.m.*

Poking against the windows was a someone with two sticking-up ears and a fuzzy face with a black spot in the middle of its forehead. Fleabiscuit!

I couldn't sit still. My knees started jumping, and my hands were having no luck trying to push them down. I had promised not to make trouble, but I could feel trouble coming. When Uncle Travis opened the door of the car and DoReMi got into the backseat, I pictured having a pacemaker like Mr.

Muffin that would make my heart beat like it was supposed to.

It took Fleabiscuit only a second to realize who was sitting in the front seat. He started making a commotion, carrying on in the plastic case, yelping and yowling and trying every dog thing to get out. He yipped and barked and tried pushing his paws against the screen, and he cried, really *cried*.

"What's up with this pooch?" DoReMi asked Uncle Travis.

"It's my nephew," Uncle Travis said. "They've got a thing going. Fleabiscuit is daffy about Nicky."

DoReMi lit up a cigar. He blew some smoke through the air of the car, and said, "Well, that's too bad. We got a long trip ahead of us, so he'd better *badword* get over it."

thirty two

I didn't want to get to the airport. I hoped Roebuck's car would have a flat tire or we'd run out of gas, but no. With Fleabiscuit whimpering in the back and me dying in the front, the trip was over before it even started. I saw the airplanes taking off and landing up ahead and the big green airport signs and now it really wasn't my heart after all; it was my stomach rocking and rolling. Uncle Travis pulled up to the terminal and jumped out of the car. He started pulling DoReMi's suitcases from the trunk.

DoReMi stepped out to the pavement, then reached into the car to get the kennel with Fleabiscuit in it. I noticed that Fleabiscuit was not wearing the coat Grandma had embroidered for him. Instead, he had on a big, wide, fancy collar with leopard spots and gold buttons all over it. I was sure it was too tight and that he hated it.

Fleabiscuit Sings!

Uncle Travis asked me to help carry DoReMi's bags into the terminal while he went to park the car. I walked behind DoReMi while Fleabiscuit, whimpering and barking, scratched at the windows of the carrying case. He'd managed to turn his body around inside it so he was looking right at me. "Aren't you going to do something?" his eyes were asking.

My stomach was doing nosedives.

The terminal was packed with people. They were streaming by with suitcases and packages, heading to every corner of the world. I followed DoReMi to the place where he would check his luggage. I saw the airline people putting suitcases on a conveyor belt. Everything on the belt would be dumped into the the freezing-cold, dark bottom of the plane. That's when I had a horrible thought: *What if DoReMi tossed the case with Fleabiscuit inside onto the conveyor belt like it was just a piece of freight?*

That did it, I guess. When DoReMi took a minute to look at his watch, I moved forward to get a closer peek at the kennel. How could Fleabiscuit survive in there? He couldn't! That's when I spotted the latch holding the door closed. My stomach lurched and so did I. I leaned forward, dropped the bags I was carrying, grabbed that latch, and as hard as I could, snapped open the little kennel door!

It all went so fast that DoReMi didn't realize what had happened until it was too late. I did see him let go of the kennel in shock, and although his cigar stayed in his mouth, his hat flew off his head. He had hardly any hair. Fleabiscuit leaped out of that plastic case like he'd been ejected by a high-tension spring. He took a quick solo flight into the air and then landed next to my feet. I jet-propelled forward like I was being chased by killers. Fleabiscuit was right there at my heels as if we were glued together. We flew through the terminal with DoReMi's voice yelling, "Hey! Hey! Stop them!" booming after us. People stopped to look but seemed too surprised to get in our way. I could have picked Fleabiscuit up then and carried him through one of the glass doors, maybe disappeared into the parking lot, if it weren't for my stomach. Nine Hope cookies were too much, I guess; there was a wastebasket, the only real piece of luck I'd had so far today. Our escape came to a screeching halt. With Fleabiscuit right at my side, I leaned over the trash basket and threw up.

A minute or two later, I heard a whistle and feet pounding toward me. I saw security guards on my right and left, and one of them scooped up Fleabiscuit and with both hands tried to get his collar off. I felt a hand on my back and another on my arm, and all this was a blur because I was still feeling sick. I couldn't have given anyone so much as my name, which is what everyone was asking for.

By the time Uncle Travis arrived, there were three more security people and at least two policemen and a crowd in a circle around us. Someone led Uncle Travis and me down an escalator and into a hallway and through a door, and we wound up in a room with a bunch of chairs around a table. A man was sitting there with a tape recorder and another one was talking on the phone. A lady was sitting at a computer typing away. The good thing was that they gave me some Coke and ice in a cup. I started to feel better, but we did have to answer about a hundred questions. It was the first time I saw Uncle Travis come really close to crying since Dad's funeral. One of the men at the table gave him a tissue so he could blow his nose. I knew what my uncle was thinking: If Dad's cap had been on his head, none of this would have happened. When the people in the room finally believed we were not mixed up with DoReMi and let us go, Uncle Travis told me he'd never take it off again.

The rest you may know from reading the papers. When I ran off with Fleabiscuit, DoReMi dropped the kennel, and one of the security men picked it up and gave it a good going over. When he opened the bottom, he found a whole big bunch of "white mosquitoes." That's what they call it when they don't call it "whizbang" or "dynamite" or just plain drugs. DoReMi also had money stashed in the fake bottom of his suitcases—the money that was supposed to be paid to the United States government in taxes. Of course, he never did get on board that plane. He was arrested on the spot and everyone thanked me for helping to capture him. It turned out DoReMi was not only taking Fleabiscuit overseas to give concerts and charge a ton for tickets, but also to get some of his "white mosquitoes" past security in a dog's fancy leopard collar.

By the time we left the airport, I felt pretty good. More than pretty good, in fact. I was carrying Fleabiscuit in my arms and sitting right up there on a cloud—cloud nine, to be exact.

thirty three

I couldn't take Fleabiscuit home, of course, but Roebuck said he'd keep him for me until we moved into our own place.

Roebuck liked Fleabiscuit's company when he was driving, and most days he picked me up after school. It meant I got to see Fleabiscuit every afternoon. We rehearsed on the roof until Fleabiscuit learned to sing "Santa Lucia." It was as if he finally decided he'd make an effort, knowing it was a surprise for Mama.

On the day of our first Grand Central concert, Roebuck came for us. He stuffed my xylophone and the rest of our gear into the trunk. Then we all crowded into the silver car, with me and Emmie, Fleabiscuit, Mama, and Uncle Travis crammed in the back, and Grandma up front with Roebuck. We had to keep the windows wide open so she wouldn't sneeze. Today Uncle Travis was wearing not only Dad's cap but his college graduation ring as well, which Mama let him borrow for the occasion.

We set up under the big MUSIC UNDER NEW YORK banner right in the main terminal. I was so excited Mama said my eyes were throwing off sparks. Mama had clipped Emmie's hair with two barrettes that blinked pink lights on and off like her shoes. I'd had a haircut and polished my shoes. Mama wore her best long dress and her earrings that glitter like they came out of diamond mines. When Roebuck took a picture of us lined up in front of some fancy stone steps in the station, he said, "You're some cool family," and I was proud as anything.

Then, as we posed for the picture, Uncle Travis happened to look up. He let out a yell and pointed at the blue-green ceiling way over our heads. "The sky!" he cried. An artist had painted figures of the constellations—a ram, a crab, a couple of fish—and my uncle was pointing to a horse with wings. A bright spark on its front legs shone like the brightest of stars in a night sky. It was almost as if it were streaming light right down on us.

Roebuck put down his camera. We all craned

our necks to check out the above.

"It's a flying horse! Just like the one on Daddy's cap!" Emmie said.

"Pegasus! He's up there!" Uncle Travis cried, and then his voice turned to a whisper. "He's here! He's watching!"

Mama put a hand on Uncle Travis's shoulder. Her eyes were focused on the ceiling too. Even Fleabiscuit's chin went up. "It's just a painted sky; it's not real," she told him, but my uncle wouldn't listen.

"There, don't you see it? It's different from all the others. It's bright. It's *him*!"

Of course, he meant Dad. I wanted like anything to believe him, but Mama shook her head and moved off to adjust her microphone. "Let's sing," she said, and our concert began.

Emmie was getting better at the flute, but it was when she danced to my playing "La Bamba" that people really applauded, as usual. When Mama did her solo of "Blue Skies," I saw a man put his arm around his girlfriend and give the top of her hair a kiss. Three people came over to buy tapes, and quite a few dropped dollar bills into our basket. We had sold about four tapes and a CD when we decided it was time for Fleabiscuit to make his debut. Mama gave me the microphone and I introduced him. "My dog's name is Fleabiscuit, and he sings. He really does!" I said.

My voice came out sort of halfway between a tenor and a baritone, but it didn't creak once. I sounded like a person instead of a log being split, and I could see people heard and understood me clearly. Not that they believed that Fleabiscuit would actually open his mouth and carry a tune as well as any singer in a church choir, no. I read people's faces, their little you're-kidding smiles, and the way they looked at each other with the oh-yeah-show-me expressions, their eyebrows raised as far as they could go.

"Ready, Fleabiscuit?" I asked, confident as anything, and I struck up the opening chords of "Danny Boy" on my xylophone. I hoped this would be the last time I'd have to use the school mallets. As Emmie blew into her flute, I imagined in about a minute Fleabiscuit would come through, the money would come pouring in like we'd never imagined, and by next week or the week after, we'd be rich.

I was right, and in some ways, I was wrong.

When Fleabiscuit began singing, I was too busy striking keys to give my full attention to the audience, but out of the corner of my eye I could see that there were more and more people crowding around us. There was a definite zing of excitement in the air. People were snapping photos, smiling, tapping their feet, and humming along. Whenever I could raise my head from the keyboard long enough to look, I saw the expressions on people's faces had changed from *You've-got-to-be-kidding* to *I must-be-dreaming*!

Fleabiscuit sang "Danny Boy" better than ever. He followed it up with "When Irish Eyes Arc Smiling" and ended with "Too-Ra-Loo-Ra-LooRal." When he'd finished, I picked him up and we took a bow together. His tail was wagging like it was charged and the crowd cheered like crazy. There was foot stamping, whistling, yells, and calls of "Bravo!" Then, more applause. People shook their heads, saying, "I didn't believe it till I saw it!" There were questions like, "Is he real? What kind of dog is that? Where did you get him?" which I tried to answer. People rushed up to buy tapes and CD's—twenty-two in all!—and to throw bills and change into our straw basket. It was full to the brim. We'd definitely made more than we'd ever made before in a single afternoon.

A flash went off. Roebuck was taking more pictures. I'd send one to Ziggy and a whole bunch to Mr. Muffin. And I'd thank Mr. Muffin like 999 times.

Someone yelled, "Encore!" and that's when I began playing "Santa Lucia."

Fleabiscuit sang along. He put his doggy heart into it. He only messed up one tiny little bit in the middle. I saw Roebuck hand Mama his handkerchief, and the next thing I knew her chin was up and she was looking at the ceiling sky and blowing her nose like crazy. Emmie was looking up at the fake sky, too, just where Uncle Travis had pointed, and she said, "He's here, Mama. He is. And it's so good. It's *splendid*."

Mr. Muffin's Hope Cookies
(Make these cookies with adult supervision.)

Ingredients

3 cups flour
1/2 cup sugar
2 sticks butter or margarine, unsalted
pinch of salt
2 egg yolks
1/2 cup butterscotch bits
2/3 cup white chocolate bits
1 teaspoon vanilla
2 tablespoons hot water (more or less)
1/2 cup confectioner's sugar
Dash of hope

Directions

- Pre-heat oven to 350 degrees.
- Smush together the first five ingredients until you have a ball of dough.
- Cover it with plastic wrap.
- Sprinkle a pastry board or flat surface with flour.
- Take a rolling pin or can of soup and roll out dough as flat as a pancake.
- Cut the dough with a buttered cookie cutter or the buttered bottom of a glass to make round shapes— about two inches across.
- Grease a cookie sheet or cover it with a sheet of aluminum foil. Place the circles of dough on the cookie sheet.

- Bake cookies for 10-12 minutes. Don't let them get brown — just a tiny bit around the edges.
- Remove from oven and cool.
- While the cookies are cooling, place the butterscotch bits and white chocolate bits in a glass measuring cup.
- Stick them in the microwave until they're mushy (about a minute).
- Add the vanilla. If the mixture seems hard, add hot water, a little bit at a time.

- When cookies are cool, remove from cookie sheet. Spread the mushy mixture between two cookies and press them together.
- Fill a pie dish with confectioner's sugar and add the dash of hope. Roll the cookie sandwich in the confectioner's sugar, shake it, and set it on a plate.

Enjoy!

Yield: Approximately 12 yummy cookies